A King Production presents…

A Titillating Tale

Mastermind…

A Novelette

JOY DEJA KING

ISBN 13: 978-1-958834-39-8
ISBN 10: 1-958834-39-4
Cover concept by Joy Deja King
Library of Congress Cataloging-in-Publication Data;
A King Production
Mastermind...A Titillating Tale by Joy Deja King
Typesetting: www.anitaart79.wixsite.com/bookdesign

For complete Library of Congress Copyright info visit;
www.joydejaking.com
Twitter @joydejaking

A King Production
P.O. Box 912, Collierville, TN 38027
A King Production and the above portrayal log are trademarks of A King Production LLC

This Novelette is Dedicated To My:

Family, Readers and Supporters.
I LOVE you guys so much. Please believe that!!

~ Joy Deja King ~

A special THANK YOU to my amazing sister
Robin, for being the inspiration for this
titillating tale.

~ Joy Deja King ~

"It Was All My Design
'Cause I'm A Mastermind ..."

A KING PRODUCTION

A Titillating Tale

Mastermind...

A Novelette

JOY DEJA KING

Chapter One

"Mr. Richardson, please come with me," the doctor said, gesturing for Cartier to follow him and a nurse into a room at the hospital.

"How is my wife? Is she getting better?" Cartier asked, concern in his voice as the nurse shut the door behind them.

"I'm afraid I have some unfortunate news to share. Despite our best efforts, Lila has passed away," the doctor informed Cartier somberly.

"I'm sorry doctor, why are we here... where

is my wife?" Cartier demanded, in denial, refusing to believe a word the doctor said.

"Sir, my name is Cynthia Johnson," the nurse spoke up, introducing herself formally. "I've been treating your wife during her recent visits. I can take you to see her, but Lila is no longer with us," she said gently, placing a comforting hand on Cartier's shoulder. "We know this isn't easy, and we're here to support you in any way we can."

"I'm sorry, Mr. Richardson, but I have another patient I need to attend to," the doctor explained. "But if you need anything, Cynthia is available to assist you," he added before leaving.

Cynthia sat down next to Cartier and asked, "Is there anything I can get for you? Would you like to see your wife?"

"I don't want to see Lila like that. I want to remember my wife for the beautiful, vibrant woman that she was. Not..." his voice cracked and trailed off.

"I completely understand," Cynthia said sympathetically. "But I do need you to sign some papers so we can release her personal belongings to you." She handed him a pen and the documents from a manilla envelope.

As Cartier signed the papers, he felt the weight of reality sink in. He remained sitting in the empty room, his face buried in his hands. Cynthia tried to offer comfort, but there was nothing she could do to ease his pain. As a nurse, she had delivered news of loved ones' deaths many times before, but it never got any easier. She always took a deep breath before entering a room, knowing that what she was about to say would change someone's life forever.

Cartier looked up with a distant gaze in his eyes. "What am I going to do without my wife? She's the love of my life." He paused and then corrected himself. "She was the love of my life." He swallowed hard, finally accepting that Lila was no longer with him.

Six Months Later...

"Cartier, our clients will be here in fifteen minutes. Do you want to have the meeting in your office or the conference room?" Callie, his Senior Marketing Executive, asked.

"Let's use the conference room. Please make sure Audra has everything set up and ready. I don't want any delays," he said while reading through some key points he wanted to address during the meeting.

"Actually, Audra is currently training a temp that was sent over to cover for Rachel."

"The receptionist... What happened to her?"

"No idea. Audra mentioned that Rachel called early this morning, saying there was a family emergency, and she needed a few weeks off. Audra's busy with the temp, so I'll have Donovan double check to ensure everything is prepared."

"Just get it done," Cartier said dismissively without looking up from his work. "And close my door."

Callie let out a frustrated sigh as she left Cartier's office. "Audra, can you please wrap up this training and meet me in the conference room? I have more important tasks for you to do." She snapped.

"Of course, Callie. Just give me one moment." Audra gave a polite smile before rolling her eyes once Callie was out of sight. "That woman is so annoying. Just because she's fuckin' the boss, she thinks she's the queen bee."

"Wow, I wasn't expecting that tea to be spilled," Serenity chimed in as she settled into her seat at the receptionist desk. "Especially since I'm only here through a temporary employment agency, so technically I don't even work here."

"That's true, which makes it even easier for me to freely run my mouth," Audra laughed. "Sorry not sorry, but Callie is truly a piece of work. The moment Mr. Richardson's wife died she pounced on him like a dog in heat. And mind you, he was screwing two other women who worked here. Both of them ended up getting fired because Callie thought eliminating the competition would increase her chances of becoming the next Cartier Richardson."

"How long ago did his wife pass away?"

"Lila passed away about six months ago. She was so young; it was unexpected and heartbreaking."

"And he's already involved with three different women?" Serenity asked in shock.

"Yes, and three is all that worked in this office. Mr. Richardson has quite the reputation as a ladies' man. Some say his behavior escalated after his wife passed away as a way to cope with his grief. Others claim he always had multiple women in rotation but was more discreet when his wife was alive."

"Interesting. Well, I'm just here to do my job and stay out of any drama," Serenity replied, eager to start working. "I need the paycheck, not the gossip."

"Girl, I feel you, but I need the paycheck. drama and the gossip," Audra laughed. "Working here is like being in a real-life soap opera, and I love it," she grinned before noticing her boss and his right-hand man walking towards them. "Good morning, Mr. Richardson and Mr. Upton!"

Both men responded dryly with a simple "good morning."

"Do you know where Callie is?" asked Cartier, looking slightly vexed.

"Yes, she's in the conference room," Audra replied, her smile never faltering as she maintained her professional demeanor.

"Thank you," said Cartier, hurrying off in the direction of the conference room.

"If you're not in the know, that's our CEO, Cartier Richardson. And the distinguished gentleman walking with him is Bradley Upton, a key player in our company's success. Some say he's really the brains and moral center behind it all, but his loyalty to Cartier never wavers," explained Audra to Serenity.

Serenity found herself completely focused on Bradley Upton. She was curious about his connection to Cartier for various reasons but kept her thoughts to herself in front of Audra. Instead, she directed her comments towards Cartier specifically.

"Mr. Richardson certainly looks the part. That suit he's wearing must have cost a grip," Serenity observed, taking note of the flawlessly tailored Kiton two-piece suit in tonal plaid, with its sharp notched lapels and white-stitched cotton pocket square. The overall look was effortlessly stylish, thanks to a casual navy Kiton cashmere-blend crew-neck t-shirt worn underneath. Dripping with a few brilliant cut diamonds, Cartier definitely knew how to flaunt his wealth.

"Oh yeah," Audra agreed. "Mr. Richardson plays no games when it comes to fashion. He only wants the best." She paused, realizing they needed to finish their conversation later. "But I better get going to the conference room before I get in trouble for gossiping too much. I'll check in on you later though. You have my cell number if you need anything," she said with a wink before rushing off.

As Serenity tried to process everything, she had learned that morning about Cartier Richardson and Bradley Upton, her phone began ringing non-stop.

"Looks like it's going to be a busy day," she said, feeling a mix of nervousness and excitement about what awaited her at her new job.

Chapter Two

Collide

"I can't believe I'm just now getting off work," Serenity muttered as she slammed the car door shut and collapsed back into the driver's seat. She took a moment to close her eyes and collect herself, thinking about how unexpected it was to be working overtime on her very first day. Turning on some music, Beyonce's "6 Inch" filled the car. With one hand on the gear shift, Serenity put the car in reverse and began to back out of the parking spot in her white 2007 Volkswagen

Jetta mouthing along to the lyrics of the song, lost in her own thoughts.

Six inch heels, she walked in the club like nobody's business.
She murdered everybody and I was the witness
She works for the money, she work for the money
From the start to the finish
And she worth every dollar, she worth every dollar
And she worth every minute
Stars in her eyes
She fights for the power, keeping time
She grinds day and night
She grinds from Monday to Friday
Work from Friday to Sunday, oh
She gon' slang
She's too smart to crave material things
She pushing herself day and night...

"Shit!" Serenity exclaimed, slamming her fist on the steering wheel as she felt her car collide with something. She quickly put the vehicle in park and got out to assess the damage. Her heart raced when she saw the 2024 Mercedes-Benz

S500 with a chrome grill and noticed white paint from her car decorating its matte black exterior. Just as she was kneeling to examine the scratch, the owner of the car approached her.

"I just bought this car, and now it's fucked."

"I am so sorry! I didn't see you behind me. Please forgive me," Serenity pleaded, standing up to face the driver. As soon as she recognized his face, she froze. "Mr. Richardson," she gasped at a loss for words. "Please don't call the agency and have me fired."

Cartier hesitated for a moment before placing her face. "You're the receptionist from the temporary agency." Serenity could see the wheels turning in this head as he considered what to do.

"Yes, sir. It was my first day. Please don't let it be my last," Serenity begged, stepping closer and briefly touching his hand. "I really need this job," she stuttered, feeling a cold breeze hit her chest. She looked down and realized that some of the buttons on her shirt must have popped open when she bent down earlier. Her ample cleavage was now on full display, with only a thin layer of lace covering them. She quickly began to button her shirt back up while continuing to apologize for the small scratch on his car.

"Excuse me…what's your name?"

"Serenity."

"Serenity, you don't need to keep apologizing. It's clear you've had a long day. Take care of yourself and drive home safely."

"But shouldn't I give you my insurance information?"

"No, it's not necessary."

"And what about..."

Cartier interrupted her, already knowing her next question. "You still have your job," he reassured her. "I'll see you tomorrow."

Serenity got back in her car, feeling relieved. The situation turned out much better than she expected. She drove off, looking forward to returning to work in the morning.

Arriving at his luxurious penthouse in the heart of Buckhead, Cartier opened the custom iron and glass French doors, that flowed into the sprawling great room. The high tray ceilings were adorned with exquisite chandeliers, while the oversized picture windows offered breathtaking views of the Atlanta skyline. He closed the motorized solar shades and drapery before pouring himself a glass of bourbon and making his way to the bedroom. As he entered the lavish primary suite, a warm fire was crackling in the stone fireplace and a familiar face was lounging in the sitting area.

"Callie, what are you doing here?" he exhaled setting down his glass of bourbon on the nightstand.

"What sort of greeting is that? I thought you would be happy to see me after our exhausting day at work."

"And I thought you returned my key. Yet, here you are," he replied coolly.

"I did return your key, but I made an extra copy that I forgot to give back," she smirked, standing up from her chair to showcase her naked body. Her five-inch heels clicked on the heated marble floor as she sauntered towards Cartier.

Callie's almond-shaped nails glided across his lips, teasing him. "Don't you think two weeks is long enough? This pussy misses you," she whispered in his ear, while using her other hand to massage his dick.

Without a word, Cartier gripped Callie's neck and pulled her towards him, sticking his tongue down her throat. He then threw her onto the bed, pulling her ass back by the waist as he undressed, thrusting his dick inside her. Callie gazed back at him with lust in her eyes, crying out his name as he filled her insides. She couldn't resist Cartier. He was her one obsession. No matter how many times he rejected her, she always found a way to get back in his bed. In her mind, having a piece of him was better than nothing at all. Plus, Callie believed that if she continued to prove herself as his loyal "bottom bitch," she would eventually graduate to being Cartier's first lady.

Chapter Three

Getting Closer

"Good morning, Audra," Cartier said stopping at the receptionist desk

"Good morning," Audra greeted with a nod.

"Serenity..." Cartier paused, glancing down at his watch. "I have to take a call, but can you come to my office in fifteen minutes?"

"Absolutely, Mr. Richardson. I'll be there."

"Did you fuck up already?" Audra noticed Serenity's eyes widen with concern. "Just kidding!" she laughed, nudging her arm playfully.

"Well, maybe I did. When I was leaving work yesterday, I accidentally hit his car," Serenity confessed.

"Damn! You definitely fucked up. A man and his toys...Cartier has plenty of them, and his cars are prized possessions."

"Do you think he'll fire me?" Serenity asked anxiously.

"I hope not," Audra sighed. "Rachel won't be back for a couple weeks. If he does fire you, I'll have to call the temp agency and go through the hassle of training someone new," she complained, rolling her eyes. "Your fifteen minutes are up. Go find out your fate."

"Mr. Richardson, is now a good time?" Serenity timidly poked her head through the partially open door.

Cartier gestured for her to enter his office as he finished up a phone call. Serenity took in the expansive view of Midtown Atlanta through the wall of glass, that flooded the space with natural light. The office was meticulously designed, blending European architecture and contemporary elements which was evident in every detail - from the black and white marble floor to the elegant bookshelves and cozy seating area with a mini bar.

"You can close the door," Cartier instructed, ending his call.

"Listen, about last night...I'm really sorry," Serenity began, but Cartier interrupted her.

"That's not why I called you in here. What happened last night was just an unfortunate accident. But because I'm understanding of your situation, I'm hoping you can do me a favor in return."

"It depends on what the favor is," Serenity scoffed, sounding offended.

"Do you think I'm hitting on you?" Cartier asked with a laugh, raising an eyebrow and standing up from behind his desk.

"No, I didn't think that." Serenity quickly responded nervously.

"Yes, you did. But I wasn't. I actually wanted to give you an opportunity to make some extra money while helping me out. You mentioned last night that you really need this job, so I assume you need to make money."

"Yes, that's correct."

"Well, every year I hold a Valentine's Gala The company staff and important business associates are invited, along with clients. My wife used to be the hostess for the event, but unfortunately, she is no longer with us."

"I'm sorry to hear about your loss."

"Thank you. Her presence is greatly missed, but I know she would want me to continue this tradition. I was thinking that perhaps you could take on the role of hostess for this year's gala. That is, if you don't already have plans with a boyfriend or anything like that."

"No, I don't have a boyfriend?" Serenity quickly clarified. "And I don't have any plans either. But I have to say, I'm surprised that you want me to be the hostess."

"Why is that? As the receptionist, you have to handle multiple tasks at once. At first, I was considering having Rachel as the hostess, but she had to take some time off. However, after our encounter last night, I think you'll be perfect for the role. You come across as very personable, and it's beneficial for both of us. Having you take over as hostess saves me from scrambling to find someone at the last minute, and it allows you to earn some much-needed extra money. So, what do you say?"

"Yes! And you're absolutely right, the extra money is much needed. It's difficult doing everything on my own, but I've never been afraid of hard work. So, any side jobs are truly appreciated. Thank you so much for this opportunity!" Serenity beamed.

"And thank you as well; this helps both of us."

"It certainly does. Now I should probably get back to my desk. Audra must be tired of covering the phones for me," Serenity said lightly.

"Oh! One more thing," Cartier added before she left his office. "This gala is very upscale, so there is a strict dress code. Formal attire is required. Will that be a problem for you?" he asked.

"No, that won't be a problem at all," Serenity smiled sweetly, closing his office door behind her.

"Finally, your back!" Audra let out a sigh of relief. "The phones have been ringing nonstop. Please tell me Mr. Richardson isn't letting you go for the day."

"No, I'm staying for the rest of the day," Serenity assured her, excusing Audra and taking her seat. "And no, I didn't get let go. You could say I got a one-time promotion," she laughed.

"A promotion?" Audra scrunched up her face in confusion. "But you don't even work here. How did you manage to get promoted?"

"Perhaps promotion isn't the right word," Serenity corrected herself. "Mr. Richardson has asked me to host his Valentines' Gala," she announced proudly.

"Seriously? His wife always hosted that event, and now he's asking you...I'm kind of offended," Audra huffed clutching at her necklace.

"Why would you be offended?"

"Because you don't even work here."

"I know, and you don't need to keep reminding me," Serenity rolled her eyes.

"I can't help it, the boss gave you this high-profile gig and it's only your second day on the job."

"To be fair, he was actually going to ask the receptionist I'm filling in for, but she's not available. I also may have mentioned how desperate I am to keep my job because I need the money, after my little incident with his car," Serenity admitted sheepishly.

"I guess that makes sense," Audra cautiously conceded. "But just so you know, this is a very upscale event. Your messy bun and those polyester pants won't cut it."

"Mr. Richardson already mentioned that to me, but thanks for the reminder," Serenity snapped back defensively.

"I wasn't trying to offend you. I'm just trying to look out for you. Answering phones is one thing, but being the hostess at our company's biggest party of the year is another level. If you need something to wear, we're probably around the same size. I'd be happy to lend you one of my dresses," Audra offered kindly.

Serenity paused her work and looked up at Audra, who was standing on the other side of her desk. Despite the slightly insulting delivery, she could tell that Audra genuinely had good intentions. "I know you're just trying to be helpful, and I appreciate it, but I'll be fine. I promise not to embarrass the boss," she said with a wink before returning to answering phone calls.

Chapter Four

"Hello, handsome! I couldn't wait to come into the office and see my sexy boss," Callie teased, as she snuck up behind Cartier.

"Please, let's not do this here," he exhaled deeply, removing her hand from his Tom Ford croc-printed leather t-buckle belt.

"Why not? We're going into your office," Callie purred.

"But we aren't in my office yet. Someone might walk by and see us," he said, leading the way towards his desk.

"We're in your office now," Callie smiled closing his office door and locking it. "Now let me taste and kiss that beautiful dick of yours." She bit her lip seductively as she moved towards Cartier.

"Not now. I have a lot of work to do," he stated firmly.

"After last night, I thought you'd be eager to be inside of me again," Callie protested, pulling on his tie as she sat on his lap and lifted her skirt.

"You thought wrong," Cartier responded, gripping her wrists tightly.

"When your wife was alive, you couldn't keep your hands off me. But now that she's dead...."

"Don't talk about Lila," Cartier chided, cutting, Callie off.

"Fine!" she snapped back," standing up. "I won't talk about Lila. But I want to know what's going on with us. You're worried about someone seeing us together at work like it's some big secret that we've been intimately involved for the past two years. And now you don't even want me to suck your dick. What the fuck is up with you? Have you found someone else?" Panic laced Callie's words.

"No, I haven't found anyone else. But it's time for you to move on," he advised.

"I'll never move on from you, Cartier. You're the only man for me, and I'm the perfect woman for you. I've proven that time and time again. I'll give you your space, but you'll come back to me. You always do," Callie said confidently.

Bradley entered Cartier's office with a heavy sense of suspicion. "Am I interrupting something?" he asked.

"No, not at all. Come in," Cartier responded calmly, barely glancing up from his documents. "Callie was just on her way out."

Bradley's gaze lingered on Callie as she quickly made her exit before turning to face Cartier again. "I thought you ended things with her?"

"I did," Cartier reiterated, with a hint of impatience in his tone.

"Then why does it feel like there's still sexual tension between you two?" Bradley pressed, not backing down.

"You're reading too much into things," Cartier dismissed with a wave of his hand. "Your analytical mind is a tremendous asset when it comes to business. Focus on that."

"So you're telling me that you haven't been sleeping with Callie for the past few months?"

Bradley's skepticism was evident.

"That's exactly what I'm saying," Cartier replied without any qualms.

"I'll take you at your word. But remember, continuing to be involved with someone like Callie could cause trouble. There are still rumors about Lila's death and we can't afford any scandals right now," Bradley cautioned.

"You worry too much," Cartier assured him, turning on his charm. "Trust me, there won't be any issues with Callie. Our relationship is strictly professional. Let's focus on what truly matters - making money."

Callie left Cartier's office consumed with fury. She tried to keep her composure as she walked down the hallway, but inside she was seething with anger. She leaned against the wall and took a deep breath, trying to calm herself down.

"Are you okay?" Donovan's voice broke through her thoughts, and she opened her eyes to see him standing in front of her.

"I'm fine," she replied, trying to push away her frustration.

"You don't look fine. Your face is all scrunched up. How many times have I told you, frowning like that causes premature aging? Keep it up and you'll start getting wrinkles," Donovan shook his head disapprovingly.

"Donovan, you sound like my mother instead of my Executive Assistant," Callie winced.

"I'm just trying to help," he said, crossing his arms. "You don't want to show up to business meetings looking like someone's great aunt when you're young enough to be their cousin. Stress can do that to you."

Callie let out a deep sigh. "Come with me." She grabbed Donovan's hand and pulled him into her office, closing the door. "I don't know what's going on with Cartier," she complained, throwing her hands up in frustration.

"Aren't you two supposed to be done?"

"In theory, yes." Callie paused for a moment before adding, "But we never really were."

"So, you enjoy having your heart stomped on by a man who won't even claim you?" Donovan shook his head with disdain. "You were carrying on with Cartier while he was married. Then his wife dies, and he still won't acknowledge you as his woman."

"Excuse me!" Callie's eyes widened, astounded by Donovan's blunt honesty.

"I recognize that look. Yes, you're my boss,

but we were friends first. That's who I am speaking to right now," he said, walking over to the built-in bookcase and staring at a framed photo of them together at last year's Valentine's Day gala. "Remember when I was dating Joseph?"

"Of course, I remember. He had a hold on you."

"Yes, he did. My ego wouldn't let me admit it back then, but a year later with a clear head, I can't deny the truth," Donovan exhaled. "It got to the point where the only time Joseph would answer my calls was if he wanted something from me."

"Oh, trust me, I remember. He was draining all your money. That's why I stepped in and offered you this job. I had to save you before you ended up broke, on the streets and moving in with me," Callie joked.

"Slow down! I still have plenty of money," Donovan quickly corrected his friend."

"You know I was kidding...well, about the going broke part," she laughed.

"But seriously, I can admit that you offering me this job saved me from a bad breakup. I needed something to distract me from Joseph because there were many times when I wanted to beg him to come back. But your bossy attitude kept me busy, but in a good way. I genuinely enjoy working for you," Donovan smiled.

"Thank you. You are hands down the best Executive Assistant I've ever had, and I'm sure I'm the best boss you've ever had."

"I know where this conversation is headed, but we need to stay on task," Donovan stated sternly. "The point I'm trying to make is that just as you correctly noticed Joseph had a hold on me, Cartier has a hold on you. It's time for you to take off your rose-colored glasses and admit the truth before you fall off the edge."

Callie quickly interjected, "My situation with Cartier is not at all like the one you had with Joseph. This great job I have, making a shit load of money is because of Cartier. He isn't using me for my funds or gifts, and to pay his bills like your ex did to you."

"Maybe that's true, but let's be real. I know what kind of person Cartier is, and he's definitely used you in more ways than just for sex. I don't need to hear all the details; even though I'm gay, I'm still a man. He doesn't keep a woman around without getting something he finds valuable in return. And once he's done with them, he tosses them aside just like he's doing to you now."

Donovan's words struck a nerve with Callie.

She turned away, not wanting him to see the pain, inner turmoil, and secrets she was hiding. Taking a deep breath and composing herself, she faced Donovan again with a stoic expression.

"Don't worry about me, Donovan. Our relationship is mutually beneficial, and I can handle myself. Now let's focus on work," cutting off any further discussion on the topic.

Chapter Five

The Gala

As Serenity made her entrance at the Valentine's Day gala, it felt like time stood still and all eyes were on her. She was a sight to behold in her form-fitting red dress that accentuated her curves and showcased her sculpted body flawlessly. The intricate beadwork that adorned the gown glimmered under the soft lighting, giving off a surreal and magical vibe as if stars were descending from the sky onto her body. Her jet-black hair fell in elegant waves, framing her face and cascading down her back. She was a vision of perfection. It seemed every pair of eyes lingered on her as she gracefully moved through the room.

"You owe me, darling," a sultry voice whispered in Serenity's ear. She turned to see Audra, who had a mischievous smile on her face.

"What do I owe you for?" Serenity asked, confusion lacing her voice.

"Just teasing, but seriously whoever helped you with your gorgeous dress, hair, and makeup deserves all the credit. You look stunning, I almost didn't recognize you!" Audra exclaimed.

"Thank you. I'll be sure to let them know. But I'm here to work, not socialize. Mr. Richardson gave me strict instructions to follow."

"Of course, carry on then. Enjoy your weekend and see you Monday at work," Audra giggled as she watched Serenity walk away.

"Who were you just talking to?" Calle asked as she and Donovan approached Audra.

"That was Serenity. She's the temporary receptionist filling in for Rachel."

"How can a receptionist afford to wear a Valentino Garavani couture dress?" Callie wondered out loud.

"You'll have to ask Serenity," Audra shrugged

nonchalantly and walked away disappearing into the crowd.

Donovan leaned in and commented, not hiding his appreciation. "That is one delectable receptionist. Not really my type though."

Determined, Callie grabbed onto Donovan's arm and they weaved through the crowd towards the welcome podium. Serenity stood there with poise and greeted each new arrival with a warm and inviting smile. As Callie approached, Serenity greeted her with the same warm smile and handed her a brochure for the gala. However, Callie dismissed it without looking.

"I don't need one of these," she snapped, slamming the brochure down on the podium. "I'm a senior executive at this company."

Serenity's smile faltered for a moment before she regained her composure. "Of course, my apologies. Well, I still hope you have a wonderful time at the gala."

But Callie's icy gaze remained fixed on Serenity as she narrowed her eyes. "You're just the temporary receptionist, right?"

"Yes," Serenity replied cautiously.

"Then who gave you permission to act as the hostess?" Callie demanded; her voice vibrating with anger.

Serenity remained composed as she politely stated, "Mr. Richardson did."

Donovan tugged on Callie's arm, trying to get her attention, but she was too focused on interrogating Serenity. Suddenly, he leaned in and whispered in her ear. "Cartier is approaching."

Callie looked up to see Cartier walking towards them. "Let's move over here," he said sternly.

Donovan stood nearby, observing as Cartier and Callie engaged in what appeared to be a heated conversation.

"What the hell are you doing?" Cartier asked unable to hide his irritation.

"What does it look like? I was talking to the temporary receptionist. Why did you hire the help instead of a professional for this year's gala?" Callie barked at him.

"I can hire whoever I want. I own this company."

"Your late wife was the one who used to host this event. Now, you're entrusting low-level employees with it?"

"I don't want to discuss this with you right now. But let me remind you to act appropriately, Callie. Show some decorum," he responded angrily before storming off.

Donovan noticed the tension and approached Callie once Cartier had left. "Are you okay? Things seemed pretty intense over here."

"I'll be fine. I can handle dealing with Cartier. What I can't handle is unwanted competition. And there's something about this woman that feels like a threat I can't ignore. A woman who looks like her doesn't end up working behind a reception desk without a motive. There's something else at play here."

Serenity was exhausted after being on her feet all night. She had no idea that playing the dutiful hostess would require so much work. Her fatigue almost made her ignore her phone until she saw who was calling. Serenity answered taken aback by the unexpected contact.

"Cynthia, I didn't think I'd hear from you tonight," she remarked. "The gala went smoothly, in case you were wondering," Serenity assured her.

"Are you positive? We can't afford any mistakes."

"I know," Serenity responded as she kicked off her six-inch heels upon arriving at her car. "Have some faith."

"You know how vital your role is. My faith comes from you being prepared," Cynthia stressed. "I'm calling because I wanted to give you a heads up; Bradley Upton will be your new point person within the company starting Monday."

"No way. How did you manage to convince him to switch sides?" Serenity asked.

"Don't worry about it. Just get some rest over the weekend, because starting Monday you'll have a new position as his personal assistant. Arrive early. Bradley will meet you in his office. Don't be late and be prepared to follow his lead. He's on our team. Stay safe, Serenity."

"Of course. And please stop worrying, Cynthia."

"I will continue to worry until this is over. I suggest you worry too. You know what happened to Lila. Don't let it happen to you," she warned.

As Serenity ended her call with Cynthia, she caught a glimpse of her reflection in the rearview mirror. Her appearance exuded confidence, but deep down she knew she was entering dangerous territory and there was an underlying fear that she might fail or even worse, end up dead.

She tried to suppress that fear, forcing her voice to sound strong and determined as she spoke with Cynthia. The gravity of what was coming next weighed heavily on her psyche, wondering if she could pull this off. But despite it all, Serenity remained resolute in her mission and nothing or no one would stop her.

Chapter Six

Playing Chess

Serenity's heels clicked against the marble floor, a staccato rhythm that echoed off the high ceilings as she approached the heavy mahogany door. She paused just outside, taking a deep breath to compose herself, the scent of her own floral perfume mixing with the more potent notes of leather and cologne that oozed in the air. Pushing the door open, she stepped into the sanctum of Bradley Upton's office.

The room was awash in the muted gold of

the morning sunlight, which streamed through the tall windows and danced across the sleek surfaces. Bradley Upton, his silhouette outlined against the brightness, turned to face her. Serenity could feel the heaviness of his gaze, analytical and searching, as their eyes met—a silent understanding passing between them.

"Good morning, Serenity," Bradley said, his voice the embodiment of calm control. "Please, take a seat."

She chose a leather chair opposite his desk, noting its plush comfort with the cool touch of the armrests. Despite the luxury that surrounded her, there was an underlying tension, like a string pulled taut, ready to snap.

"Let's begin because I want to go over a few things with you this morning before anyone comes into the office," Bradley stated, settling himself into his chair. He leaned forward, hands clasped, his gray hair catching the light and lending him a distinguished air that matched his precise mode of speech. "Understanding the hierarchy within CR Enterprises is crucial. It's like a chessboard; every piece has its function. And just like in chess, if you observe carefully, you can predict the next move."

Serenity nodded, her focus entirely on him,

aware that this lesson could mean the difference between success and the ultimate failure.

"Each department, each team lead... they're all part of a larger structure, one that Cartier has meticulously built." Bradley gestured subtly with his hands, drawing an invisible map in the air. "The more you understand how Cartier's mind operates when it comes to business; the easier you'll be able to maneuver in his world."

Serenity lifted her hand, mimicking a student in a classroom seeking permission to speak.

"Please forgive the interruption, but I have to ask. Why have you turned against Cartier? You've worked by his side for years, and from what I heard, you've always been blindly loyal. Your sudden change is perplexing to me."

Bradley's expression remained hard to read, the lines of his face etched with a mix of resolve and conflict. He leaned back in his chair, fingers steepled in front of him as he regarded Serenity with a contemplative gaze.

"You're right to question my motives, Serenity," Bradley began, his voice measured yet tinged with a hint of emotion beneath the surface. "The truth is, loyalty can only stretch so far before it becomes a shackle, binding you to someone whose actions you can no longer condone."

Serenity observed the various emotions that played out on Bradley's face. While he spoke, her expression darkened momentarily, a hint of uncertainty because of her lack of confidence in his full commitment.

"But what has changed?" she pressed; her tone gentle yet probing. "What has made you question Cartier now?"

Bradley let out a heavy sigh that seemed to carry the weight of years of unspoken truths. "It's not just about questioning him, Serenity. It's about realizing that there are lines even the closest of allies shouldn't cross. I've seen things, things that don't align with the values and principles I hold dear," Bradley confessed. "Things at play here that go beyond what I can ignore. Cartier's methods, the deals he makes, the people he associates with...They're leading him down a dangerous path, one that I can no longer stand by, and watch unfold."

Serenity leaned forward; her interest heightened by this unexpected revelation. From what she'd been told, everyone perceived Bradley as the unwavering pillar of loyalty within Cartier's inner circle, and now, seeing cracks in that facade left her curious.

"Can you give me an example?" Serenity inquired softly, her voice a contrast to the tension that hung in the air between them.

Bradley paused for a moment, as if considering the weight of his words. "There was an incident last month," he began, his tone grave. "A deal that Cartier orchestrated behind closed doors, one that went against everything we stand for. It involved... methods that I cannot condone."

"Methods like what?" Serenity's mind raced as she tried to piece together the puzzle that Bradley was beginning to reveal.

"The deal involved a rival company—a ruthless corporation with criminal ties and known for their cutthroat tactics. Cartier's willingness to align our interests with theirs, to sacrifice our values for temporary gain. He knew I would never approve, so he waited until after the deal was closed before letting me know. I cannot trust Cartier or his decisions any longer. He is not the man I once knew."

"Does that mean you agree with Cynthia?" Serenity pushed.

Bradley leaned back in his chair, placing his pen down, seeming to be extremely mindful of what he said next.

"Being an unscrupulous businessman is one thing, being a murderer is a whole other beast.

Unfortunately, I'm starting to believe Cartier was involved in Lila's passing. I want to be wrong, but I need to know the truth either way. If I am right, and he is complicit in her death, then there must be justice for Lila. She was an incredible woman."

Serenity felt a sense of uneasiness but wasn't exactly sure why. Cartier, the charismatic businessman who exuded charm and success, now had his carefully crafted image starting to shift, revealing a darker complexity.

"I need you to be cautious, Serenity," Bradley emphasized, his voice marked with urgency. "You're entering into a world that performs at the highest level of deceit where trust is a luxury we can ill afford. You have a pivotal role to play here—a delicate dance with Cartier that draws him closer to you. But one misstep could mean disaster."

Serenity absorbed his words. She took Bradley's warning seriously. She knew she had entered a realm far more treacherous than she had anticipated. As Serenity sat there, absorbing the gravity of Bradley's revelations, a sense of dread crept over her like a shroud. She pondered her decision to assist in bringing Cartier down and doubts began to form in her mind.

Bradley's words lingered in the air. Serenity

felt a surge of conflicting emotions swell within her—doubt, fear. She was about to play a dangerous game where the stakes were high.

"I am well aware of the risks," she declared her voice unwavering despite the storm of emotions churning inside her. "I am not deterred. In fact, I am more resolute than ever to emerge as the winner."

Bradley's face returned to its usual stoic mask. "Then let the preparation begin," he said, the seriousness of his words underscoring the grimness of the path Serenity had chosen.

Chapter Seven

Let The Seduction Begin

Serenity ran her fingers over the smooth, luxurious surface of the rich reddish brown mahogany desk that was a far cry from the receptionist counter she was accustomed to. The atmosphere was filled with a distinct aroma, a mixture of expensive cologne and a subtle hint of deceit. She couldn't help but wonder how many lies had filled this room, how many acts of betrayal had taken place in the lavish surroundings and the false sense of comfort provided by such opulence.

Audra confidently strode into the office, her eyes lighting up as she spotted Serenity. "Well, well, talk about a quick rise to the top," she remarked, standing in the doorway with a relaxed yet poised posture.

"Damn, you scared me!" Serenity exclaimed, jumping out of her chair.

"I come in this morning expecting to see you at the front desk and instead I find out you're now Mr. Upton's personal assistant. Number two guy at CR Enterprises. You even have your own office! How did this happen?" Audra closed the door behind her.

"Good morning to you too, Audra," Serenity said with a smile.

"Let's skip the pleasantries. I need to know all the details."

"There's not much to tell. While working as the hostess at the gala, I struck up a conversation with Mr. Upton. I mentioned that I was temporarily filling in as the receptionist and he offered me a permanent position. Of course I accepted, because the pay is great, and I know I'll learn a lot from working directly with him."

"You know," Audra paused and put a finger to her chin, "it might have been that red dress you wore to the gala. You looked incredible."

"Are you saying I got the job because of how I looked in a dress?" Serenity laughed. "Just because I started as a temporary receptionist, if you look at my resume, I'm highly qualified for this position. I just needed the right opportunity."

"I'm sorry, Serenity. I was trying to be funny, but it didn't come out that way," Audra apologized. "Listen, I really like you. I've liked you since we first met. And now, I'm thrilled that you have a permanent position here. I finally have someone I can get drinks with after work."

"I like you too, Audra," Serenity replied with a genuine smile.

Serenity allowed herself to briefly consider the possibility that Audra Thompson could be more than just a colleague - perhaps even a potential confidante in this intricate dance of danger and deception she had become a part of. She was still wary of Bradley Upton, unsure if he was fully committed to their cause. Having another person who knew all the players involved could be beneficial.

"How about we celebrate your promotion with a night out after work?" Audra suggested.

"I would love that. I haven't had a chance to explore all the amazing places Atlanta has to offer," Serenity replied.

"Perfect. There's a great spot right down the street that we can check out. Meet me by the elevators when you're done with work. See you later!" With a wave, Audra left Serenity's office.

"Oh, hey Callie," Audra said in a dry tone as she bumped into her on her way out of Serenity's office.

"Why are you coming out of an empty office? Don't you have work to do?" Callie remarked.

"Obviously you haven't heard that office isn't empty anymore. The temp who was filling in for Rachel landed a permanent position here. She's Mr. Upton's new personal assistant. Talk about lucky," Audra gloated before walking away, leaving Callie fuming.

Callie headed straight to Bradley's office armed with this new information. She barged in without bothering to knock, catching him in the middle of a phone call.

"Are you fucking the receptionist?" she hissed.

"Let me call you back," Bradley said ending his call. "What the hell is wrong with you coming into my office with this nonsense?" his tone aggressive.

"It's not nonsense. How does someone go from being a temporary receptionist to the personal assistant of the second-in-command over the weekend? Unless, of course, she's sleeping her way up," Callie snapped.

"That's rich coming from a mid-level employee who only became a senior executive by bending over backwards for the CEO."

"I earned my position in this company."

"Oh, I know. You definitely earned it by spreading your legs."

"You bastard. Don't you dare speak to me like that."

"Callie, I can speak to you however I want. You are not Cartier's wife, and you're no longer even his mistress. So, watch how you talk to me when you come into my office. Now get out," Bradley demanded.

The rage inside of Callie was boiling over, evident in her intense glare at Bradley, but he ignored her which only infuriated her even more. She stormed out of his office with even more determination to uncover everything she could about Serenity.

After work, as Serenity and Audra walked into the lounge, a wave of excitement washed over Serenity. The dimly lit space was filled with plush velvet couches, shimmering chandeliers, vibrant artwork, a massive bar adorned with crystal decanters and decadent drapes added to the ritzy venue. Every detail of the ultra-modern decor was designed to entice and indulge.

"This place looks amazing!" Serenity exclaimed.

"I knew you'd love it. They have the best cocktails here too," Audra replied, leading her towards a booth in the corner of the room.

As they settled into their seats, Audra ordered them both a round of martinis and mini gourmet desserts as they began to discuss life outside of the office. Gentle piano music was playing in the background, setting a sophisticated and alluring atmosphere. The tinkling of glasses and murmurs of conversation added to the overall air of indulgence.

Serenity took a sip of her drink and sighed. "Can you believe this is my first time going out since I've been here? Well, if you don't count the Valentine's Gala."

"Well, now that we're friends," Audra winked, "I'll be taking you to all the hotspots. Trust me, there are plenty. But, this place is perfect for meeting rich men."

"I believe it," Serenity replied as she glanced at the cocktail menu. "These prices are insane."

"No worries. Tonight's on me. I know you just started your new position at work."

"Thank you, because I was about to send this drink back," Serenity laughed.

"Don't even worry about it. Once we start going out more, guys will be lining up to pay for your drinks. Wait, I didn't even ask...are you seeing anyone?" Audra inquired.

"No, I ended things with my ex before moving here. It was one of the reasons I decided to come to Atlanta - for a fresh start."

"This city is all about new beginnings and opportunities. You'll have plenty of options here. Speaking of options, excuse me for a moment - that guy I'm interested in just walked in," Audra said with a smirk, before taking another sip of her drink and making her way over to him.

As Serenity nibbled on a mini dessert, she noticed Cartier sitting at a table across the room with another man, engaged in an intense conversation. After a while, Cartier excused himself and headed towards the restroom. Serenity quickly scanned the room to see where Audra was - she was deep in conversation with the guy she had been eyeing at the bar.

Serenity released her hair from its clip and ran her fingers through it, giving it a tousled and slightly messy look. She finished her drink, reapplied some lip gloss and spritzed on some perfume. As she made her way towards the restroom, Cartier walked out, and Serenity almost stumbled into him.

"Are you okay?" he asked, steadying her.

"I'm fine," Serenity mumbled, pretending to be drunk.

"Serenity?" Cartier said, finally recognizing her face.

"Do I know you?" she slurred, pressing herself against his chest.

"Come sit down with me," Cartier said, guiding Serenity to a nearby bench. "Who did you come here with?"

"I don't remember...I think she left. You're so cute," Serenity giggled playfully. "What are you doing here?" she asked, resting her head in his lap.

"You've had too much to drink. Let me take you home," Cartier said with concern.

Cartier drove Serenity to his home when she pretended to be too out of it to remember her address. Upon entering his penthouse, Serenity continued her act.

"I'm feeling so hot," she complained taking off her shoes and slowly removing her clothes. Finally, she was left standing in just her bra and panties before collapsing onto the sofa.

The sight of her nearly naked body made Cartier aroused. However, he resisted the temptation and grabbed a blanket from the linen closet to cover her. He thought she had fallen asleep and turned to leave.

"Can you get me some water? I'm really hot," Serenity mumbled.

"Of course," Cartier replied.

When he returned with a glass of water from the kitchen, Serenity had sat up and let the blanket slip off her body, revealing her breasts. She could see Cartier's eyes lingering on them.

"Thank you. I feel so embarrassed. I didn't realize I drank so much. This is the second time I've made a fool of myself in front of you. I hope you can forgive me again, especially with my new job position."

"Bradley mentioned he hired you as his new personal assistant."

"I was actually out celebrating my promotion. Obviously, I got carried away. You're not going to tell him what happened? Or worse, you're not going to fire me?" Serenity's expression showed fear.

"No, you weren't drunk on the job. But please be careful. A beautiful young lady like yourself, alone and heavily intoxicated, could be taken advantage of," Cartier warned.

"You think I'm beautiful?" Serenity asked innocently yet seductively.

Cartier brushed Serenity's hair out of her face. "Of course I do," he said as he traced his finger along her lips. She opened her mouth and ran her tongue over his finger.

Cartier couldn't resist the temptation any longer. He leaned in and captured Serenity's lips with his own, softly at first but then with more urgency as their kiss deepened. Serenity responded eagerly, pulling Cartier closer to her.

Their breaths became heavy as they explored each other's mouths, their tongues dancing together in a passionate rhythm. Cartier slid down Serenity's bra strap, using his tongue to tease her hardened nipple. She moaned in pleasure, arching her back and pushing herself closer to him. Cartier gently laid Serenity down on the sofa as their passion intensified. He sprinkled kisses along her neck and chest, igniting a fiery sensation with each touch of his lips. Serenity couldn't help but release soft sighs of pleasure as he continued downwards licking her clit. Serenity writhed under his touch, letting out moans and gasps of pleasure as he brought her closer and closer to the edge. Just when she thought she couldn't endure anymore, and had reached her climax, Cartier stopped and stood up. He looked down at Serenity with desire burning in his eyes.

"I want you." Serenity's voice was inviting and sultry.

She moved towards him and wrapped her arms around his neck, pulling him into another passionate kiss as she pushed him back onto the sofa. She straddled Cartier running her hands over his chiseled chest before leaning down placing the tip of her tongue on his earlobe.

Cartier moaned in pleasure as she worked her way down to his neck, leaving traces of kisses and love bites. She slid down his body, her lips trailing towards his hardened dick. Serenity unzipped his pants, revealing his hardened erection. Her eyes widened in desire as she slowly wrapped her hand around his manhood and stroked it, feeling its incredible length and thickness. Cartier savored in Serenity's touch, pulling her hair tightly taking pleasure as she took him into her mouth. She was eager to taste him and feel him inside her. She slowly slid her mouth up and down his shaft, her lips gliding smoothly against his skin.

Serenity then escalated her sex game sensing he might like it rough, and she was more than happy to oblige. She bit down gently on his pulsating vein, causing him to groan even more, urging her to continue. Cartier's hands gripping the back of her head, guiding her movements as she continued to pleasure him with her mouth. It wasn't long before he was ready to explode, his breathing becoming heavier and his body tensing up.

"I'm going to cum," he rasped, his voice full of urgency. Serenity gave him what he needed at that moment. She rose up, their eyes locking in a heated stare, and thrust herself down onto his dick. Cartier exhaled swimming in her wetness feeling himself deep inside her. Their bodies moved together rhythmically, each thrust eliciting a soft moan from Serenity. Cartier reached up and cupped her breast, rolling her nipple between his fingers as he watched their bodies come together.

"That's it, baby," she purred, "please don't stop."

She could feel the warm tingle building within her, her orgasm drawing closer with every movement. She arched her back, her hips locking against his as she felt the pleasure wash over her like an overpowering wave. Cartier groaned loudly, his body stiffened, thrusting into her one last time. Serenity felt his hot seed spilling inside her, its warmth spreading through her. They both stopped moving, their bodies still joined as they caught their breaths together. They lay there, basking in the aftermath of their intense lovemaking. Their eyes met in the dimly lit room, filled with a fusion of lust and satisfaction.

"That was... intense," Serenity whispered, still trying to catch her breath.

Cartier held her gaze for a moment before breaking into a smile. "It was more than intense. It was... perfect," he said brushing Serenity's hair out of her face.

"You're right. It was perfect," she smiled back at him. Cartier's gift for business was equally matched by his gift in the bed. However, Serenity knew this was not the time to get dickmatized. She had to remain focused on her plan to uncover the truth. But for the moment, they lay wrapped in each other's arms as she savored the afterglow from their lovemaking.

Chapter Eight

Shatterproof

Serenity's sexual escapades with Cartier continued to dominate their lives over the next several weeks. To the point, he struggled to resist his
desire to taste her even while on the job. Serenity had to force him to slow down so they didn't
raise any eyebrows at work. Occasionally they
would disappear into his office to steal kisses but
only briefly. However, today Cartier was out for
a business meeting, and she used his absence to
her advantage. Her heart pounded as she slipped
into Cartier's office. A sense of nostalgia encom-

passed her as the scent of his expensive cologne lingered in the air. She instantly had flashbacks of them having mind blowing sex last night on his penthouse terrace. The warm breeze hitting their bodies with each thrust. She paused, snapping out of her thoughts listening intently for any sign of movement in the hallway outside. "Silence. Perfect."

Her eyes darted around the room, taking in the sleek mahogany furniture and plush leather chairs. Sunlight streamed through floor-to-ceiling windows, casting long shadows across the polished marble floor.

"Focus," she whispered to herself, pushing away memories of Lila consuming her thoughts. There would be time to grieve later. Now, she needed evidence.

Serenity moved swiftly to Cartier's imposing desk. She pulled open the top drawer, rifling through immaculately organized files. Nothing incriminating yet, but she couldn't give up. Lila deserved justice. As she searched, Serenity's mind raced. How could a man so charming, so successful, be capable of such evil? She remembered the first time she'd met Cartier, how his intense gaze and confident smile had an almost hypnotizing effect.

"Appearances can be deceiving," she muttered, carefully replacing each document exactly as she'd found it. A soft sound from the hallway made her freeze. Footsteps? No, just the hum of the air conditioning kicking on. Serenity exhaled slowly, willing her racing pulse to calm. She moved to a tall filing cabinet, methodically examining each drawer. Her fingers brushed against a folder labeled Confidential Acquisitions. "Interesting." She carefully photographed its contents with her phone, making sure to capture every detail.

Serenity's eyes widened as she scrolled through the encrypted emails on Cartier's computer. Her heart pounded in her chest, each decrypted message revealing more of the sinister plot that had claimed Lila's life.

"Ain't this some shit," she muttered under her breath, her fingers flying across the keyboard. "They really planned it all out," Serenity exhaled shaking her head in disgust.

As she worked, Serenity's mind was flooded with memories of Lila - her infectious laugh, her unwavering kindness. The grief threatened to overwhelm her, but she pushed it down, channeling it into fierce determination. A particularly chilling message from Callie caught her eye:

"Once she's out of the picture, everything will be ours."

Serenity's stomach churned. She took a deep breath, steadying herself against the wave of nausea and anger that washed over her. The stark reality of Lila's murder, so coldly discussed in these emails, made her blood boil.

"You heartless bastards," she whispered, her voice trembling with barely contained rage.

Serenity's thoughts drifted to Callie. That auburn-haired temptress who Cartier had wrapped around his finger. She plotted against Lila because she was desperate to take her place.

Her eyes then fell on a small safe tucked behind a row of leather-bound volumes. Jackpot. But how to crack it? Before she could contemplate further, the unmistakable sound of Cartier's voice drifted through the door. Panic surged through her veins as she scrambled to return everything to its proper place. "Fuck! he wasn't supposed to be back for at least another hour," she fumed under her breath.

"...meet me in my office in five minutes," Cartier was saying, his tone clipped and authoritative.

Serenity's heart threatened to burst from her chest as she made a final sweep of the room, ensuring nothing was out of place. She slipped out the side door just as Cartier's hand closed around the main entrance's doorknob.

Safe in the hallway, she leaned against the wall, struggling to catch her breath. She hadn't found a smoking gun, but she was one step closer. For Lila's sake, she would keep digging until the truth was revealed.

Serenity flinched at the sudden sound of Callie's voice. "What were you doing in Cartier's office?" she demanded an answer, her tone imposing.

Serenity refused to be intimidated by Callie's aggressive approach. "I was dropping off some paperwork for Mr. Richardson, as requested by Mr. Upton. When I saw that he wasn't there, I left."

"Stop lying," Callie snapped.

"Why don't you tell me what your problem is, Callie?" Serenity asked, trying to diffuse the tension.

"You're my problem. I don't know what game you're playing, but I'll figure it out and get rid of you," Callie threatened. But Serenity refused to engage in Callie's threats and instead chose to walk away. However, Callie wasn't done yet. She stormed into Cartier's office, insisting they talk.

"I just caught that Serenity woman coming out of your office while you were gone. I can feel that she's up to something dangerous. You need to get rid of her," Callie advised Cartier.

"I'm sure she had a valid reason for being in my office," Cartier replied calmly.

"She claimed she was dropping off paperwork to you from Bradley, but she didn't have anything in her hands except her phone. Why would she lie unless she was doing something sneaky?"

"Callie, you're getting worked up over nothing. Serenity is harmless."

"Please! She's probably been hired by one of our competitors to gather intel on us. I'm going to make some calls and prove it."

"There's no need for that," Cartier interrupted.

"Yes, there is!"

"No, there isn't!" Cartier retorted, locking his office door behind them.

"That woman gives me a bad vibe. She wants to sabotage this company and I'm going to expose her."

"No, you're not going to do anything," Cartier stated firmly. "Serenity is not trying to harm this company."

"You don't know that!" Callie fumed.

"Yes, I do," Cartier replied confidently.

"How?"

"Because we're involved," he admitted.

Callie's face was drenched in shock, drained of all color. "What do you mean by 'involved'?" she asked, her voice trembling.

"I think it's pretty clear," Cartier replied, not wanting to elaborate on their relationship any further.

"You're fucking her? You can't be serious. This woman goes from being a receptionist to Bradley's personal assistant, and now she's sleeping with the CEO within a matter of weeks. This can't be real," Callie ranted, pacing back and forth in disbelief.

"Callie, I have to meet with Richard. Please use discretion and keep my involvement with Serenity between us for now," Cartier instructed, unlocking his office door and ushering a stunned Callie out. "Richard, come on in."

Across town, Cynthia sipped her latte at a trendy

café, her eyes scanning the bustling street outside. Her curly hair bounced as she turned to greet an approaching figure. "Melissa! Thanks for meeting me," Cynthia said, her warm smile masking the tension beneath.

Melissa was a mutual friend of Callie and Lila. She slid into the seat across from Cynthia. She seemed to want to be anyplace but here. "Of course. Though I'm not sure how much help I'll be."

Cynthia leaned forward, her voice low and conspiratorial. "Any information about Callie could be crucial. You've known her longer than most."

Melissa fidgeted with her napkin. "Callie's always been... enigmatic," she said, choosing her words carefully. "Even back in college, she had this way of charming people, especially men in positions of power."

Cynthia's eyebrows raised slightly, her mind racing. "Like Cartier Richardson?" she probed gently.

Melissa's eyes widened. "How did you know about that? Callie made me think their relationship was a well-kept secret."

Cynthia kept her composure. "Just piecing things together. Besides, I think their romantic relationship was actually the worst kept secret at CR Enterprises. How deep does their connection go?"

"Do you think Lila knew?" Melissa wanted to know with guilt filling her eyes.

"I'm sure she did," Cynthia reasoned.

"I thought we were close. She never mentioned it to me. If Lila knew, she must've died believing I betrayed her. I feel horrible." Melissa put her head down, clearly overwhelmed in grief.

Cynthia reached her hand across the table. "You can still make it right. Tell me what you know."

As Melissa began to divulge details about Callie's past, Cynthia's thoughts drifted to Serenity, hoping she was having luck in her own investigation.

Serenity retreated to her office after her confrontation with Callie to examine the evidence she found in Cartier's office. As she tried to piece together the puzzle, her phone began to vibrate insistently. She glanced at the screen and saw

Cynthia's name flashing, so she picked up without hesitation.

"Serenity, you won't believe what I've found out," Cynthia's voice came through, excitement and dread mingling in her tone.

"Spill it," Serenity replied, her eyes still glued to the computer screen.

"I've been digging into Callie's past, and girl, it's dark. She's got connections to the Peachtree Syndicate."

Serenity's breath caught. The Peachtree Syndicate was notorious in Atlanta's underworld, known for their ruthless tactics and far-reaching influence.

"Are you sure?" Serenity asked, her mind racing with the implications.

"Positive. I've got a source who swears Callie's been their inside woman for years. It explains how she and Cartier have been able to operate under the radar for so long."

Serenity leaned back in her chair, the weight of this new information settling heavily on her shoulders. "This is bigger than we thought, Cynthia. I'm looking at emails right now that spell out exactly how they planned to take Lila out."

There was a moment of silence on the other end of the line. When Cynthia spoke again, her voice was thick with emotion. "We're going to make them pay, Serenity for what they did to Lila."

Serenity's heart pounded as she decrypted another email. "It's like putting together a twisted jigsaw puzzle," she muttered, half to herself and half to Cynthia.

"What are you seeing?" Cynthia's voice crackled through the phone; tension evident in her tone.

Serenity's eyes narrowed as she scanned the decrypted text. "They used code names. Cartier is 'The Architect' and Callie is 'The Siren.' They discuss Lila as 'The Obstacle.'" A wave of nausea washed over her as she read further. "Dear God, Cynthia, it's so cold. They planned every detail."

"Those bastards," Cynthia hissed. "How could they do this to her?"

Serenity's mind raced, piecing together the fragments of information. "The Peachtree Syndicate connection explains their resources. But why Lila? What did she know?"

"I'm still working on that," Cynthia replied. "My source is skittish. Says Callie's got eyes everywhere."

A chill ran down Serenity's spine. She glanced around her office, suddenly feeling exposed. "Be careful, Cynthia. We're dealing with dangerous people. I thought maybe this was simply a love triangle that turned deadly but it's so much more."

"I know and we're bringing everyone involved down. So, you be careful too, Serenity. Don't take any unnecessary risks."

As Serenity ended the call, she couldn't shake the feeling that she was being watched. The significance of their discovery pressed down on her, a combination of triumph and terror. She thought of Lila, of the life stolen from her friend, and that steeled her resolve.

"We're coming for you," she whispered to the silent room, her fingers returning to the keyboard with renewed purpose.

Chapter Nine

In Too Deep

The glittering chandeliers at Atlanta's most exclusive country club cast a warm glow over the sea of designer gowns and tailored tuxedos. Cynthia smoothed down her emerald silk dress, her heart racing beneath the calm exterior she fought to maintain. She had gone from being a clinical nurse specialist to a novice sleuth doing background and forensic investigations. The change was daunting, but it was for an excellent cause. Her eyes scanned the crowded ballroom, searching for her target.

"Marcus Rawlins! Look at you, it's been years!"Cynthia smiled affectionately. His dark hair perfectly coiffed, a crystal tumbler of scotch in his manicured hand. Cynthia's pulse quickened. This was her mark – Callie's former college confidante and the key to unlocking her mysterious past.

Marcus eyed the attractive woman who was impeccably dressed, trying to see where he knew her from. "My apologies, how do I know you?"

"Me and Melissa would hang out with you sometimes when we would visit Callie at school. You know Callie Morgan."

"Oh yes. Now I remember. You did used to come visit her at college," Marcus pretended to remember thinking it must be true. "You're still beautiful I see. How have you been?"

"Wonderful and you?" as they engaged in small talk, Cynthia's mind raced. How could she steer the conversation towards Callie without raising suspicion?

"I heard you're still in touch with Callie," she ventured, keeping her tone light. "She's become quite the social butterfly, hasn't she?"

Marcus's eyes flickered, a shadow of unease crossing his features. "Callie? Yes, we keep in touch," he replied, his tone guarded. "She's certainly come a long way since our college days."

Cynthia sensed his hesitation and pressed gently, "Oh? So, she wasn't always able to sway and influence people to get things done her way. I thought maybe she was born with that gift," Cynthia teased.

Marcus took a long sip of his scotch, his gaze darting around the room as if checking for eavesdroppers. "Well," he began, lowering his voice, "I'm sure you remember that Callie wasn't the polished socialite we see today."

"True, she has become a bit smoother with her moves," Cynthis agreed.

"I guess that's one way of putting it. She had... connections. Dangerous ones. That's how Callie swayed things in her direction." Marcus shot Cynthia a knowing nod.

Cynthia kept her expression neutral. "Connections? How intriguing. Do tell."

As Marcus spoke in hushed tones, Cynthia's mind reeled. Callie's involvement with drug cartels, her sudden disappearance senior year, the unexplained influx of cash, it all painted a chilling picture of a woman with a dark past and even darker secrets.

Meanwhile, on the other side of town, Serenity cautiously made her way through the hallways of CR Enterprises. The late hour meant she was likely the only one there, but her nerves were still on high alert.

She slipped into Cartier's office with a master key Bradley gave her. Serenity's eyes swept the room, searching for anything out of place. That's when she spotted it – a tiny lens glinting in the carved molding above his desk.

Serenity's breath caught in her throat. A hidden camera. With a steady hand, she retrieved the compact hacking device from her purse and connected it to Cartier's computer.

"Come on, come on," she muttered, watching the progress bar inch forward as it downloaded the camera's footage. Suddenly, voices echoed from the hallway. Serenity froze, her heart pounding. She quickly disconnected the device and slid it into her pocket, just as the office door swung open.

Her heart raced as she turned to see Cartier standing in the doorway, his dark eyes narrowing as they landed on her.

"Serenity," Cartier said, his voice like velvet over steel. "What are you doing here?" his tone remained deceptively calm, belying the underlying tension that crackled in the air between them.

Serenity met Cartier's gaze with steely resolve, a mask of cool composure settling over her features as she rose from the chair, her stare unwavering. "I could ask you the same question, Cartier," she replied smoothly, her mind working furiously to come up with a plausible explanation. She couldn't afford to show any sign of weakness.

Cartier circled around the desk, his movements deliberate and predatory. "You haven't answered my question," he murmured, stopping behind her. Serenity could feel his breath on the nape of her neck, sending shivers down her spine.

"I was snooping...," Serenity stepped back, turned around and faced Cartier.

Cartier's sharp features were etched with surprise and suspicion by Serenity's admission. "You're spying on me, looking for something incriminating?" his words hung heavy in the air.

"Yes. The other day I had a run in with Callie. She saw me coming out your office. I was checking to see if you were back from your meeting because I wanted to surprise you. Of course I couldn't tell Callie that. She became completely hostile. By her reaction, it was obvious she was jealous. It made me think that maybe you all were involved romantically. You've tried to have sex with me in your office a few times and I declined. I thought maybe Callie did what I wouldn't do."

"So, you came in here looking for evidence that I had sex with Callie?"

"I saw her exit your office today when I was leaving work. It raised my suspicions. Are you having sex with Callie? Because she seems to be very territorial of you."

"No, I'm not having sex with Callie."

"Then why did she look like she wanted to punch me in my face when she saw me coming out your office? First, she accused me of having sex with Bradley to get my job, then she explodes if I have any interaction with you. Cartier, I need you to tell me the truth because honestly, I'm falling for you, and I don't want to get my heart broken. If you're seeing Callie, I need to know."

Cartier let out a heavy sigh. "I used to be involved with Callie, but it's over. I promise."

Serenity hung her head as if she was devastated by his admission, and that this new disclosure hurt her. Cartier gently lifted her chin and looked into her eyes.

"I want to believe you, but..."

"No buts. I'm with you," Cartier said, leaning

down to kiss Serenity. "You don't have to snoop around my office looking for proof."

"I'm sorry. I know I shouldn't have done that. But when I saw Callie coming out of your office, all these thoughts rushed through my mind, and I let my jealousy take over."

"You have nothing to be jealous about."

"You promise?"

"Yes, I promise," Cartier assured her.

Relief filled Serenity. She managed to change the optics. Instead of being caught digging for information to bring Cartier down, he believed she was an insecure lover.

Cartier's lips met hers. His touch ignited a fierce desire within Serenity. She responded to him, their connection melting away what she initially came there for, leaving only the raw intensity of their shared moment.

"I want you to make love to me," Serenity said moving the items cluttering Cartier's desk aside and leaning back, inviting him to fulfill her request.

With practiced precision, Cartier lifted Serenity onto the edge of the desk, his movements confident and commanding. Their kiss was a flurry of emotions – longing, need, and a hint of vulnerability beneath the surface. The scent of his cologne mingled with the heady aroma of craving his touch, created an intoxicating blend that enveloped them in a haze of lust.

As they moved together in a dance of desire and need, the world outside faded away, leaving only the two of them giving into their sexual desires. Serenity felt herself falling deeper under Cartier's spell, surrendering to the overwhelming connection that bound them together. In that intimate moment, as their bodies became one, Serenity found solace, and their lovemaking was a tumultuous blend of raw desire and unspoken emotions, each movement a silent promise of understanding and bonding. Serenity clung to Cartier as if he were her lifeline, the boundaries between them blurring into a haze of shared intimacy. As they lay entwined in each other's arms, the world outside seemed to disappear.

Callie's determination to get rid of Serenity had only intensified. She suspected that the former front desk receptionist had secured her promotion by sleeping with Bradley. But after

Cartier confirmed their romantic involvement, she found herself unable to sleep at night.

In the darkness, Callie's silhouette and fiery auburn hair were visible as she walked into the warehouse. A tall, muscular man stepped out of the shadows to greet her.

"You're late," Callie grumbled, her typically smooth voice laced with annoyance.

"Traffic," the man grunted. "Do you have the money?"

"It's all there," Callie confirmed. "Now, about Serenity..."

"I don't need a refresher," the man cut in. "If I can't dig up any dirt on her, I'll fabricate some."

A cold and humorless laugh escaped from Callie's lips, filling the warehouse. "Good. That sneaky bitch won't be causing me any further problems."

The man nodded, a predatory glint in his eyes, pocketing the envelope of money Callie handed him. "Consider it done. I'll make sure Serenity won't cause you anymore trouble. She'll be out of your life."

Callie watched him with a calculating gaze, her mind already plotting the downfall of her perceived rival. "How about making it permanent," she instructed, a cruel smile playing on her lips, handing over additional funds for motivation.

With a subtle nod, the man took the extra cash, the exchange sealing their sinister alliance.

"As always, discretion is paramount. I trust you'll handle it with your usual... finesse," Callie emphasized.

The man slipped back into the shadows, leaving Callie alone in the eerie silence of the warehouse. She turned to leave, the echo of her heels against the concrete floor reverberated through the empty space, a haunting cadence that lingered her thoughts consumed by vengeance and power. She relished the idea of Serenity's demise, seeing it as the final step to securing her position to be back at Cartier's side. With a flash of malice in her eyes, "Let the games begin," Callie whispered to herself.

Chapter Nine

The Unthinkable

Cynthia and Serenity met at a diner just outside Atlanta in a back corner booth to avoid any potential sightings.

"How did everything go when you snuck into Cartier's office the other night?" Cynthia asked, taking a sip of her coffee.

"I almost got caught, but I was able to think quickly and come up with an excuse," Serenity confessed.

"That had to be some excuse. What exactly

did you say?" Cynthia was curious to know.

"When he walked in on me, I told him I was feeling insecure about his relationship with Callie and was snooping around to see if they were involved. We ended up having sex and all was forgiven." Serenity shrugged.

Cynthia gave her a skeptical stare and leaned back in her seat. "Are you sure you're not falling for Cartier?"

Serenity let out a nervous laugh. "Of course not. It's all part of the plan to get close to him and gain his trust."

"True but using real emotions like insecurity and sex...it seems like you're getting too deep into this role," Cynthia pointed out. "And don't forget why we're doing this."

"It worked, didn't it?" Serenity said defensively, "And believe me, I haven't forgotten what they did to Lila."

"Listen to me. I've been around Cartier. His charm is undeniable. When I met him, it was hard for me to even fathom he was capable of killing his wife. But while I was treating Lila, we became close, and she confided in me. He is diabolical. We must get justice for our dear friend who they mercilessly murdered. Don't ever forget that." Cynthia stressed.

"Lila's memory is a constant presence in my mind. We grew up together in the foster care system, almost like sisters. We shared the same foster parent when we were younger, a nightmare that eventually led us to being placed in different homes one after another. Our shared experience bonded us, making sure we always had each other's backs. Until one day, Lila disappeared. It was devastating and I felt completely alone without her. I constantly wondered what happened to her until you called me with the news of her death," Serenity spoke with a heavy heart. "So yes, we must seek justice and ensure Cartier and Callie pay for what they've done."

"I'm glad to hear you're still all in. It's easy for lines to get blurred when emotions become involved," Cynthia acknowledged.

Serenity slid the USB drive across the table. "Here you go. All the important evidence is contained on the drive - footage of illegal deals and email exchanges planning Lila's murder."

"We've got them now," Cynthia said triumphantly, a hint of delight in her voice.

"I know. We can finally make them pay for what they did," Serenity nodded, feeling both relieved and anxious about their next steps.

"But how do we use it without putting ourselves in danger? These people are capable of anything." Cynthia's voice trailed off as she noticed Bradley approaching their table.

"Sorry I'm late," he said, joining them at the booth.

"No worries. Serenity just gave me the USB drive with all the evidence she retrieved from Cartier's office," Cynthia informed him.

"Excellent work," Bradley praised Serenity. "This is going to be crucial in taking down Cartier and Callie," he affirmed.

The trio sat in tense silence for a second, each lost in their thoughts as they contemplated the gravity of their mission.

"We have to be careful how we proceed," Bradley cautioned, glancing around the diner discreetly. "Cartier and Callie will fight back, and they have resources at their disposal that we can't underestimate."

Cynthia nodded in agreement, her eyes darting between Serenity and Bradley. "We'll have to strategize our next moves meticulously. One wrong move could jeopardize everything we've worked for."

Bradley leaned in; his expression serious. "I have some contacts in the police department that might be able to help us. We can anonymously tip them off with the evidence on this USB drive and let them handle the investigation."

Serenity hesitated, weighing the options carefully. "It's risky. What do you think Cynthia?"

Before Cynthia could respond, Bradley's phone buzzed with an urgent message. His expression darkened as he read it, and he quickly turned to face them.

Bradley was brief and to the point. "We have a problem," he said sharply. "Callie is aware of the evidence, but she doesn't know who's in possession of it. Once she discovers the identity of the holder, she plans to send someone to intercept it before they have a chance to take action."

"Are you sure...how?" Serenity questioned.

"Yes." Bradley confirmed.

"From what I learned about Callie, her connections run deep. There is no telling how she was alerted," Cynthia sighed.

Serenity's heart raced at the news of Callie's potential interference, a cold dread settling in the pit of her stomach. Her mind contemplating how to outmaneuver her cunning adversary. She exchanged a worried glance with Cynthia, the gravity of the situation sinking in.

"We have to act fast, Bradley. Is there any way we can neutralize Callie and safeguard the evidence?" distress filled Serenity's words.

Bradley nodded; his resolve evident. "I'll investigate who is responsible for bringing the evidence we obtained to Callie's attention while you two search for a secure location to hide the USB drive until we decide our next move."

Cynthia's expression hardened as she reached for the USB drive, her fingers gripping it tightly. "We can't risk losing this. It's our best chance at achieving justice for Lila." Determination flashing in her eyes. "I have a secure spot where no one would think to look."

Serenity and Bradley watched Cynthia, a sense of relief washing over them as she took charge of the crucial evidence. Her confidence was reassuring in the face of looming danger.

"Ladies, I need you to be careful," Bradley emphasized. "I'll be in touch as soon as I uncover who is feeding Callie information and how much she actually knows."

Cynthia and Serenity nodded in agreement before Bradley left.

"Do you think Bradley will be able to figure out who leaked the information to Callie?" Serenity asked.

"Callie has some powerful associates, but so does Bradley. I trust that he'll uncover the truth.

In the meantime, we need to be cautious and I'm going to make sure to protect our evidence."

"I have dinner plans with Cartier tonight but call me if you need me to help you with anything. I'll make myself available."

"With everything going on, you think that's wise?" Cynthia's frown showed her disapproval.

"Bradley said Callie doesn't know who has the evidence, so I need to act normal around Cartier or he'll start suspecting something," Serenity explained.

"Just be careful. We all know what Cartier is capable of," Cynthia warned before they both left the diner and went their separate ways.

The soft glow of candlelight danced across Serenity's face as she gazed at Cartier from across the table. The intimate ambiance at one of Atlanta's most exclusive French restaurants, enveloped them in a cocoon of luxury and romance. Cartier's deep brown eyes locked onto hers, a smoldering intensity in his gaze that sent a shiver down her spine. He reached across the table, his fingers brushing against hers as he lifted her hand to his lips.

"Have I mentioned that you look absolutely breathtaking tonight." Cartier spoke in a low and hypnotic tone staring at Serenity, who was wearing a rose gold v-cut top with a matching belt worn at the waist tucked into a rose gold slip skirt with strappy open toe heels. She accessorized her look with embellished hoop earrings, sleek updo, and a nude glossy lip.

"Yes, but you can keep telling me; I never tire of hearing it," Serenity blushed admiring how appealing Cartier looked in his immaculately tailored navy suit that accentuated his broad shoulders. She didn't want to feel so sexually drawn to him, but it was proving to be difficult.

As Cartier's thumb traced lazy circles on her palm, Serenity leaned in closer. The attraction between them was undeniable, electric. But she couldn't let herself get distracted from her true purpose.

Cartier flashed a charming smile. "You know, this is our first official date."

Serenity couldn't help but playfully tease him. "Really? With all the intimate dates we've shared in the privacy of your place, I didn't even realize." She grinned. "But I must admit, it's nice to dress up and have a romantic dinner with you."

Cartier chuckled, a rich, warm sound that seemed to reverberate through her. He nodded in agreement. "We should definitely do it more often. There's still so much for you to learn about me. I'm full of surprises."

If only you knew, Serenity thought, maintaining her mask of intrigue and desire.

"I would like that," Serenity said, her smile widening.

"Then that's what we'll do." Cartier reached across the table to place a small velvet box in front of her. "I love seeing that smile on your face. And I hope this will make it last even longer."

Serenity's eyes sparkled with excitement. "You got me a gift!" She clapped her hands with delight. "I don't know what to say."

"You can open the box and let me know if you like it." Cartier suggested.

Serenity laughed nervously. "Yes, I think that would be a good idea."

She slowly opened the velvet jewelry box and gasped at the sight of the stunning diamond tennis bracelet inside.

"I can't believe you got this for me." She was too overwhelmed to even put it on.

"Allow me." Cartier took the bracelet from

the box and gently fastened it around her wrist. Serenity could only stare in awe at the beautiful piece of jewelry as Cartier looked on with a satisfied grin.

Donovan was the first to spot Cartier and Serenity sitting at a table as he stood by the entrance. He considered coming up with an excuse for them to leave, before Callie noticed the couple, but it was too late.

"Do you see that shit?!" Callie exclaimed in shock. "I can't believe he would bring her here. How dare that motherfucker!"

"Calm down, Callie," Donovan quickly said, scanning the upscale restaurant for prying eyes. "Let's not make a scene."

"It's already too late!" Callie retorted, marching straight towards Cartier's table.

"Callie, please stop!" Donovan called out after her, but she ignored him and kept walking. He hurried to catch up.

"Are you serious! Bringing the hired help to this elegant restaurant and buying her expensive jewelry?" Callie seethed as she caught sight of Cartier clasping a diamond bracelet around Serenity's wrist.

"This isn't a good idea. We should leave," Donovan strongly urged his boss and close friend.

"Let me handle this," Callie said dismissively, holding up her hand to silence him.

"You should listen to Donovan," Cartier warned. "Because you're making yourself look foolish."

"You should be utterly embarrassed of yourself! Is she sucking your dick so good that you feel compelled to parade the hired help around like she's a trophy?"

Callie's incessant chatter was background noise to Serenity as she received a text from Cynthia, urgently asking her to meet up. "Excuse me, Cartier, I have to go," Serenity interjected, grabbing her metal clutch purse.

"Let's not allow Callie to spoil our evening. We can leave whenever you're ready," Cartier responded, standing up.

"It has nothing to do with her. A friend of mine, she needs my help," Serenity explained.

"I'll take you to her," Cartier offered, concerned.

"No need, there's already an Uber waiting for me outside. I'll be fine. I'll call you later," Serenity said, rushing out before Cartier could object.

Serenity had her Uber driver drop her off in

the parking lot where Cynthia's car was parked. She then had to navigate through a narrow alley, the faint glow of flickering streetlights casting eerie shadows along the walls. "Ugh!" Serenity whispered as she debated taking off her uncomfortable strappy high heels. Eventually, she arrived at an unassuming door hidden behind stacks of discarded crates in an abandoned warehouse. The rusty hinges creaked ominously as she pushed them open. "Out of all the places for Cynthia to hide the evidence, it had to be here," Serenity grumbled as she called out to her.

Inside, the air was musty and thick with stale particles of dust. The only light came from grimy windows high above, casting a dim glow on the scene before her. Serenity made her way to a secluded corner where she first noticed Cynthia's purse and car keys. Then there she was. Cynthia's lifeless body lay next to a loose floorboard. She kneeled down and checked for a pulse. "Oh God, she's dead!" Serenity cried out in a panic, seeing the fresh pool of blood surrounding Cynthia's body. Her eyes followed the trail of blood seeping through the loose floorboard and saw a small combination safe tucked underneath. It was open and empty; Serenity knew that had to be where Cynthia had stashed the USB drive.

Serenity's heart pounded rapidly as she looked around the warehouse, searching for any sign of the missing USB drive. She knew that evidence was critical to bringing down Cartier and Callie, but now Cynthia's life had been taken in the process. Tears streamed down her face as she felt shocked, guilt, and anger. She wiped her tears away, knowing she needed to stay focus.

With trembling hands, she reached for her phone and called Bradley. It rang twice before being answered. "Hello."

"Bradley. I need your help," Serenity said urgently.

"Of course. What can I do?"

"It's Cynthia. She's dead," Serenity cried, and the USB drive is gone."

"Serenity, get out of there now! You could be in danger. I'll make sure the police locate Cynthia's body, but you don't need to be anywhere around when they arrive. Go stay at a hotel. It might not be safe for you to go home. I'll be in touch."

"Okay."

Without wasting another moment, Serenity hastily gathered Cynthia's purse and car keys as she made her way out of the warehouse, each step laden with fear. When she reached Cynthia's car, the sound of screeching tires echoed behind her.

A dark SUV pulled up beside her, and to her horror, two burly men stepped out, eyes fixed on Serenity. One of the men grunted a rough, threatening command: "Get in the car!"

Terror engulfed Serenity as the henchmen approached. She knew she had to act quickly. With sudden determination, she shoved the keys into one man's face and swung her metal clutch purse, landing a solid hit on the other man's jaw. The element of surprise was on her side, and she made a break for Cynthia's car.

As she struggled with the car door, the heavy footsteps of the men closing in sent a surge of adrenaline through her veins. Just as the first man reached out for her, she slammed the door shut, turned the key in the ignition, gripping the steering wheel tightly. Serenity's heart was thumping as she put the car into reverse and hammered her foot down on the accelerator, tearing out of the parking lot running over one of the men in the process.

As she sped away from the scene, fear and anger surging through her body, her mind was bombarded with the events of the night. Cynthia was gone, and now there were men after her.

Serenity navigated through several backstreets, trying to distance herself from the warehouse before pulling into an isolated gas station. She glanced at her phone and saw that she had missed multiple calls from Cartier. Part of her wanted to call him back, but then she couldn't shake the thought that he might be responsible for Cynthia's death. As she debated her next move, she heard a phone ringing, but it wasn't hers - it was coming from Cynthia's purse. Serenity retrieved her phone and saw an unknown caller. Something inside her urged her to answer the call.

"Yes?" Serenity attempted to disguise her voice and mimic Cynthia's tone as best as possible.

"Thank God you answered. I haven't been able to reach Bradley, have you heard from him?" the voice on the other end sounded frantic.

"No." Serenity kept her response short, hoping the caller would reveal more information. There was a brief moment of silence.

"Cynthia, is everything okay? Why are you giving me one-word answers?"

Serenity froze for a moment. This can't be happening, she thought to herself. "Everything is fine." Serenity replied before the caller hung up.

Two Years Earlier...

Chapter Ten

The Scheming Begins

The crystal chandeliers cast a warm glow over the opulent ballroom, their light dancing off champagne flutes and glittering jewels. Cartier Richardson surveyed the crowd of Atlanta's elite, his keen eyes searching for his next conquest. That's when he saw her.

She stood alone by a marble column, her auburn hair cascading down her back in soft waves. As if sensing his gaze, she turned, meeting his eyes with a look that sent a jolt through him.

Cartier felt his pulse quicken as he made his way across the room.

"I don't believe we've met," he said smoothly, offering his hand. "Cartier Richardson."

"Callie Morgan," she replied, her voice like honey. "Though I'm sure you already knew that."

Cartier raised an eyebrow, intrigued by her boldness. "And what makes you say that?"

Callie's lips curved into a knowing smile. "A man like you always does his homework."

As they bantered, Cartier found himself drawn in by her wit and charm. There was a sharpness to her that matched his own, a hunger that resonated with his deepest desires.

She could be useful, he thought, imagining the doors her beauty and cunning could open.

"Care to get some air?" Cartier suggested, gesturing towards the terrace.

Callie's eyes glinted mischievously. "Lead the way."

The cool night air was a welcome respite from the stuffy ballroom. Cartier leaned against the balustrade, taking in the twinkling lights of Atlanta's skyline.

"Beautiful view," Callie murmured, coming to stand beside him.

"Indeed," Cartier agreed, his gaze fixed on

her profile. "Though not as captivating as the company."

Callie turned to face him; her expression suddenly serious. "Let's cut the small talk, Cartier. We both know why we're out here."

Cartier felt a thrill of excitement. "And why is that?"

"Because we recognize something in each other," Callie said, her voice low. "A shared ambition. A willingness to do whatever it takes to get what we want. Something I'm sure your lovely and sweet wife is not in agreement with."

Cartier began to contemplate the endless possibilities. "And what is it you want, Callie?"

"The same thing you do," she replied, her eyes burning with intensity. "Power. Wealth. To stand atop the world and look down on all the fools beneath us."

A slow smile spread across Cartier's face. "My dear, I believe this is the beginning of a beautiful partnership."

As they plotted and schemed under the starlit sky, Cartier felt a sense of exhilaration. In Callie, he had found not just an ally, but a kindred spirit. Together, there was nothing they couldn't achieve.

And anyone who stands in our way, will have

to face my wrath and desire for vengeance, he thought, raising his glass in a silent toast to their shared ambition.

The sleek black Bentley glided to a stop in front of Riverwood Industries' gleaming headquarters. Cartier stepped out, adjusting his pristine custom suit. Callie emerged moments later, her crimson dress a stark contrast to the gray Atlanta morning.

"Remember the plan," Cartier murmured, his hand resting briefly on the small of Callie's back.

Callie gave him a predatory smile. "Oh, I remember. Poor Charles won't know what hit him."

As they strode into the lobby, Cartier's mind relished in the idea of what this would mean if all went as planned. Charles Riverwood had been a thorn in his side for far too long, blocking expansion deals and poaching key clients. But not for much longer.

The elevator dinged, depositing them on the top floor. Charles greeted them with a broad grin, oblivious to the danger lurking behind their polished facades.

"Cartier, Callie! What a pleasant surprise," he boomed, ushering them into his office.

Cartier's eyes darted around the room, cataloging potential witnesses. "Charles, always a pleasure. We have an exciting proposition for you."

As Callie engaged Charles in small talk, Cartier subtly maneuvered himself between Charles and the door. His anticipation of what would soon unfold gave him a powerful thrill.

"So, what's this proposition?" Charles asked, leaning back in his chair.

Cartier locked eyes with Callie, a silent signal passing between them. In one fluid motion, Callie produced a small vial from her purse and tipped its contents into Charles' coffee while he was distracted by Cartier's smooth words.

"We believe a merger would be mutually beneficial," Cartier proposed, watching intently as Charles took a sip of the tainted drink.

Within minutes, Charles' face paled, his breathing becoming labored. "I... I don't feel well," he gasped.

Callie's voice dripped with false concern. "Oh no, Charles! Should we call for help?"

Cartier felt a rush of dark pleasure as he watched Charles struggle. "I'm sure it's nothing serious," he said coolly, making no move to assist.

As Charles slumped over his desk, Cartier couldn't help but admire the efficiency of their plan. He caught a glimpse of Callie, seeing his own satisfaction mirrored there.

Later that evening, exuberance filled Callie's place, as they relished in seeing their plan executed without any glitches.

"We did it," Callie breathed, a hint of exhilaration in her voice.

Cartier nodded, pouring himself a generous glass of cognac. "Indeed, we did. Charles' 'unfortunate heart attack' will pave the way for our takeover."

"And what about his wife?" Callie asked, her tone sharp. "She still holds significant shares."

Cartier's eyes narrowed. "Leave her to me. I have my ways of... persuading people."

"Your ways?" Callie scoffed, jealousy igniting and her earlier elation evaporating. "And what exactly does that mean, Cartier?"

He turned to face her, sensing the shift in her mood. "It means whatever is necessary, Callie. You know that."

"Do I?" she challenged, stepping closer. "Because lately, it seems like you're making decisions without consulting me. We're supposed to be partners in this."

Cartier felt a spark of annoyance. "Partners, yes. But don't forget who brought you into this world, Callie. Who gave you the opportunities you now enjoy."

Her eyes flashed dangerously. "Is that a threat, Cartier? Because I assure you, I have my own methods of ensuring my success."

As they glared at each other, Cartier realized with a chill that the very traits he admired in Callie – her cunning, her ruthlessness – could easily be turned against him. He wondered, not for the first time, if he had created a monster he could no longer control.

Callie leaned in, nodding towards the couple on the other side of the room as the music played during the annual Christmas party at CR Enterprises. "Look at how Cartier is holding her hand and gazing in her eyes. It's like they're madly in love," she commented to Donovan.

"Well, she is his wife," Donovan remarked taking a sip of his wine.

"I still don't understand why he doesn't just divorce her. She's so dull and sweet. She'll never be enough to keep his attention. I'm a much better match for him."

"Ah, the classic mistress delusion," Donovan smirked.

Callie glared at Donovan, infuriated with his assessment.

"I am more than just Cartier's mistress. We are partners in every sense of the word. I've played a crucial role in making CR Enterprises one of the top companies in the country. Lila is not worthy of a man like him. It's time for her to go."

"Go where exactly? I seriously doubt that woman is giving up her husband."

Donovan's remark hit a nerve, but Callie masked her irritation with a tight smile. She knew her true place in Cartier's life.

"You underestimate my influence, Donovan," Callie replied smoothly. "Lila may not willingly give up her husband, but when the time is right, she'll be out of the picture."

Donovan digested Callie's words, assessing her carefully. "You never fail to surprise me, Callie. Your ambition knows no bounds but you're treading on dangerous ground. Cartier may be drawn to your fire, but he's also wary of getting burned."

Callie's jaw tensed, her nails digging into her palm. "Cartier may not see it yet, but I'm the one who truly understands him. I know his desires, his ambitions, his weaknesses. Lila is nothing more than an obstacle in our path to greatness. I know how to handle him, Donovan. I know Cartier better than anyone else. I can promise you; Lila will be out of his life."

Donovan raised an eyebrow skeptically. "And when will that be? Cartier seems quite content with the status quo."

"I wasn't born to be second best. And I won't settle for it."

"So, what's your next move? Eliminate the competition?" Donovan inquired.

A dangerous smile played on Callie's lips. "It's not competition if they don't even know they're in the game."

Donovan observed Callie. It felt like he was witnessing a pivotal moment. Her relentless drive and cutthroat desire left him wondering just how far she would go to achieve her goals.

Present...

Chapter Eleven

Bradley entered Serenity's office and closed the door behind him. "You didn't have to come in today," he said, concern evident in his voice. "After what happened with Cynthia, I thought you would want to take a few days off."

Serenity was caught off guard by Bradley's sudden appearance. "Good morning," she greeted him. "I did consider taking some time off, but I wanted to talk to you first. Something happened over the weekend that has me on edge."

"What happened?" Bradley asked, worry creasing his brow.

"When I left the warehouse two men tried to kidnap me in the parking lot while I was heading to Cynthia's car."

"What! Did they hurt you?"

"No. But it did leave me rattled. I followed your advice and stayed at a hotel for the remainder of the weekend. However, this morning, I decided the safest place for me would be an office building with lots of people around. No one would dare harm me with so many witnesses," Serenity reasoned.

"You have a point, but I'm more worried about your mental well-being. Finding Cynthia's dead body must have been traumatizing," Bradley said.

"It was," Serenity agreed. "And it all happened so quickly. One minute she's texting me to meet her at the warehouse, and the next I find her dead. This whole situation is insane. And now the USB drive with all our evidence against Cartier and Callie is gone."

"I know," Bradley sighed heavily. "We're back to square one without that USB drive."

"Do you think Cartier and Callie had something to do with Cynthia's death? We were all together at the restaurant, but they could have hired someone," Serenity shook her head not wanting to believe Cartier was involved.

"It seems likely," Bradley said grimly.

"That means Cartier might have also been involved in trying to kidnap me," Serenity's anger and confusion grew. She glanced down at the diamond bracelet on her wrist, a gift from Cartier. How could he give her such a beautiful present and then potentially harm her?

Serenity's mind was a whirlwind of conflicting emotions as she stared at the sparkling diamonds adorning her wrist. The bracelet suddenly felt heavy, a weighty reminder of the tangled web of deceit and danger surrounding her. The man whose charm had drawn her in, now loomed as a potential threat to her life.

Bradley's voice cut through her thoughts; his concern palpable. "Serenity, you need to be careful. Cartier is not someone to underestimate. If he's involved in all this, we have to approach every move with caution."

"I won't rest until I uncover the truth," Serenity's fortitude unfaltering.

Bradley placed a reassuring hand on Serenity's shoulder. "We'll find a way to get justice for Lila and now Cynthia. We just have to keep digging."

When Cartier walked into Serenity's office, he immediately noticed Bradley sitting close to her, seemingly comforting her. "Am I interrupting something?" he asked.

"Not at all," Bradley replied. "We were just discussing some things before our meeting this afternoon. If you have any other questions, let me know."

"Will do," Serenity smiled politely.

"Bradley, in case Serenity hasn't had an opportunity to tell you, we're together now," Cartier announced, to her surprise.

"Oh really, she didn't mention it," Bradley responded calmly.

"Well now you know, and soon everyone else in this office will too," he declared.

"Does that include Callie?" Bradley questioned sarcastically.

"Callie has known about my relationship with Serenity for some time. Now, if you could excuse me, I need to speak with Serenity privately," Cartier said, making it clear that he wanted Bradley to leave.

Bradley lingered at the door, observing Cartier's persuasive demeanor. He'd always had a reputation as a ladies' man, playing and manipulating women to get what he wanted. Bradley could only hope that Serenity wouldn't fall prey to his charm and would remain focused on their mission to take Cartier down.

"What was that all about?" Serenity inquired once Bradley had left, and they were alone.

"I'm not sure what you're referring to," Cartier pretended innocence.

"Making a big announcement about us being a couple," she clarified.

"Is it wrong for me to publicly declare what's mine?" Cartier gently caressed Serenity's cheek. "What happened to you over the weekend? You left me abruptly at the restaurant, then ignored my calls and texts."

"My friend needed me; she was going through a tough time. I spent the weekend with her," Serenity lied.

"How is she doing now?" Cartier asked with concern.

"Not good. Not good at all."

"I'm sorry to hear that. But I don't like not knowing where you are," Cartier shifted the conversation. "This weekend made me realize how valuable you are to me."

"What does that mean?"

"It means I want you to move in with me," Cartier asserted.

"Are you serious?" Serenity was stunned.

"Yes. I know there are still things we don't know about each other, but I believe we have something special, and we should explore it."

"I don't know what to say."

"Say yes," Cartier pressed.

"Yes," Serenity beamed.

"Perfect. I'll have the movers pack up your belongings and bring them to the penthouse."

"Just like that?" Serenity questioned.

"When I want something done, I make it happen." Cartier stated confidently. "I have a meeting to attend, but I'll see you after work." He kissed Serenity goodbye and left, leaving her feeling frustrated that she couldn't resist his charm.

"Callie, there are some documents that need your signature," Donovan announced, walking into her office catching her in the midst of being extra animated.

Callie put up her index finger, signaling for him to wait while she finished her phone call. "Get it done!" she yelled angrily before abruptly hanging up. "Why can't he just take care of this?" Callie vented.

Donovan closed the door behind him, noticing that Callie was on the verge of a meltdown. "What happened now?" he asked.

"This might be too much for you," she sighed, leaning back in her chair. "I could really use a strong drink right now."

"Should I pour you some tequila?" Donovan offered as he walked towards the bar in her office.

"Not at the moment. I need my mind lucid," Callie responded, accepting the papers from Donovan and signing them quickly. "But thanks for the offer."

"What's got you so worked up?" Donovan asked, genuinely worried.

"I don't know if you want to hear this," Callie hesitated before continuing.

"We've been friends for years. Nothing you say will shock me."

"Since you insist," she shrugged. "This man who has done a lot of work for me in the past was supposed to get rid of Serenity, but he keeps fucking up. It's driving me crazy because I can see that Cartier is falling for her," Callie grimaced.

"When you say, 'get rid,' do you mean find

her another job or...?" Donovan trailed off, hoping for a different answer.

"You know what I mean," Callie shot him a knowing look. "I did warn you that you might not want to know."

"I'm glad you told me so I can talk some sense into you. You need to let go of this obsession with Cartier. Are you going to spend your entire life getting rid of every woman he gets involved with?" Donovan sighed.

"Only the ones that matter. But eventually, Cartier will realize that I am the one for him."

"Callie, you know I've got your back. You were there for me when I was going through my horrible breakup with Joseph, and I'll always love you for that. Which is why I must be honest with you. You need to move on from Cartier, or he will be the end of you," Donovan forewarned her.

Callie heard Donovan's words, but her determination to be with Cartier was unwavering. Anyone who stood in their way had to go.

Audra caught Serenity just as she was about to

enter the elevator. She gasped and couldn't resist asking, "Girl, are the rumors true?"

Serenity responded with a coy smile, "What rumors would that be?"

"That you and the CEO are an item?" Audra asked excitedly. "It all makes sense now why you've been too busy to join me for drinks after work. You're too busy handling 'real business' with the boss."

"Well, it's not quite as scandalous as you make it sound, "Serenity laughed. "But yes, the rumors are true. We actually moved in together," she revealed.

Suddenly, Callie appeared seemingly out of nowhere, "You what!" Did I hear right? You've moved in with Cartier?"

"Callie, ear hustling is not cute on anyone," Audra frowned.

"This coming from the office gossip monger," Callie scoffed.

"Whatever," Audra rolled her eyes. "Let's go get some lunch Serenity. Callie, you're looking a little hungry, do you want us to bring back something for you?" she joked as the elevator doors closed. But this was no joking matter for Callie.

The click of her stilettos echoed through the

marble-floored hallway as she stormed towards Cartier's office. Her mind raced with memories of their relationship - the passion, the betrayal, the desire that use to smolder between them. She steeled herself, knowing this confrontation could change everything.

With a final steadying breath, Callie grasped the polished brass doorknob and twisted it forcefully. She burst into Cartier's office, the scent of his cologne enveloping her as she strode purposefully toward his imposing desk.

"What are you doing here?" his tone clipped. Annoyed by the intrusion.

Callie's face was flushed. She faltered for a moment, drinking in the sight of him. Desire and anger warred within her as she struggled to find her voice.

"We need to talk, Cartier," Callie finally managed, her words coming out in a rush. "It's about Serenity. You moved her into your penthouse? What do you even know about this woman?"

Cartier had a look of exasperation crossing his handsome features. "I thought I made it clear that my relationship with Serenity is none of your concern."

Callie's hands clenched at her sides as she fought to maintain her composure. She couldn't let him dismiss her so easily, not when so much was at stake.

"Please, just hear me out," she pleaded, taking another step closer to his desk. "I wouldn't be here if it wasn't important."

As Cartier's cold gaze bore into her. Would he even listen to her warnings about Serenity? Their shared history hung heavy in the air, unspoken but impossible to ignore.

"I hired a private detective to investigate Serenity's past," Callie disclosed. "But he found nothing. It's as if she only appeared less than a year ago."

"You did what?! How dare you violate her privacy like that?" Cartier slammed his fist onto the desk. "You've crossed a line."

"I'm trying to protect us, Cartier. She's dangerous, and you're playing right into her hands."

"There is no us. The real danger is you, Callie. My patience is wearing thin." Cartier stood up from his chair. "Serenity is off limits. If you continue with this, I'll have to take care of you myself."

"Take care of me? Who do you think you're talking to? This arrogance because of all your success is partly because of me," she reminded him.

"And I've paid you generously for your ser-vices. I made you a wealthy woman. So quit with the dramatics and move the fuck on with your life. Our relationship is strictly business now. I'm with Serenity."

"She's not the right woman for you, Cartier. None of them are," Callie protested.

"None of them except for you? Get over your-self. I don't want you anymore, Callie. Now get out of my office, and if you keep causing trouble, you'll be out of my company too," he threatened.

Callie felt her heart shatter into a million pieces at Cartier's harsh words. She had expected resistance from him, but the finality in his words cut deeper than she had anticipated. The once fa-miliar space now feeling foreign and unwelcom-ing. Her facade of confidence crumbled as tears welled up in her eyes, betraying the vulnerability she had been trying to mask. She knew their re-lationship had forever changed, but the sting of his rejection was devastating.

"You can't just dismiss me like this, Cartier!" Callie's voice rose, her eyes blazing with hurt and fury. There was fight still burning within her. She refused to be cast aside so easily, not after every-thing they had shared.

Cartier's expression hardened as he moved

around his desk, closing the distance between them with purposeful strides. "I can, and I just did. Our personal relationship is over. Now it's time for you to accept reality and move on."

Cartier's dismissal felt like a physical blow to Callie, but she refused to back down. She continued to stand her ground; with their shared history and the secrets they held between them, pressing down on her like a suffocating blanket. With a heavy heart, Callie finally turned, her heels clicking sharply against the marble floor as she made her way to the door. She paused at the threshold.

"You'll regret this, Cartier," she whispered, her voice laced with a warning and sorrow before she swept out of the office, leaving behind a stream of emotions in her wake.

As she made her way down the hallway, Donovan caught up with her, concern etched on his face. "Callie, I heard what happened. Are you okay?"

Her voice fluttered as she fought to keep the tears at bay. "I'll be fine, Donovan. Just... give me some space right now."

Donovan nodded, understanding the rawness of the wound that had been reopened. He watched her figure diminishing in the distance.

He couldn't bear to see her heartbroken again, especially at the hands of Cartier Richardson. He prayed this would be the last time.

Chapter Twelve

Blinded By Love

The flickering candlelight highlighted Cartier's chiseled features as he stared into Serenity's eyes while they relaxed in their luxurious hotel suite.

"Serenity," Cartier began, his voice subdued and hypnotic. "From the moment I first saw you, when you hit my car," he briefly laughed, "I knew you were different. Special. I never had any intention or desire to remarry after losing my first wife, Lila. But you've brought a light into my life I never knew I was missing."

A whirlwind of emotions hit Serenity. She struggled to keep her expression neutral as Cartier continued his impassioned speech.

"Your strength, your passion, your beauty - inside and out - they've captivated me completely. I can't imagine my life without you in it."

Memories of Lila when they grew up in foster care together flashed through Serenity's mind. The laughter they'd shared, the dreams they'd whispered late at night. All of it stolen away. She swallowed hard, forcing herself to push out thoughts of Lila to focus on Cartier's words.

"I know we haven't known each other long, but when you know, you know." His gaze intensified. "Serenity, I want to build a life with you. To face whatever comes our way, together."

Doubt gnawed at her. Was she strong enough to see this through? To maintain the facade while seeking the truth? Serenity's fingers twitched in Cartier's grasp, but she resisted the urge to pull away.

"You've become my world," Cartier continued. "My first thought when I wake up each morning, my last thought before I fall asleep. I love you, Serenity. With every fiber of my being."

The sincerity in his voice made her question everything she knew about Cartier. For a moment, Serenity almost believed him. She forgot the darkness that lurked beneath his polished exterior. She blinked rapidly, fighting back tears born of frustration, fear and yearning to share her life with him.

"Cartier, I-" she began, her voice barely above a whisper.

He squeezed her hands gently. "You don't have to say anything yet. I know this is a lot to take in. I just needed you to know how I feel. How deeply I care for you."

Serenity nodded, not trusting herself to speak. Her quest for vengeance suddenly felt impossibly far away, slipping through her fingers like grains of sand. Cartier's hand slipped into his pocket, retrieving a small velvet box. With fluid grace, he sank to one knee before her, his movements illuminated by the flickering candlelight. Serenity's breath caught in her throat as he opened the box, revealing a stunning diamond ring that sparkled with brilliance.

"Serenity," Cartier's voice was low, intimate. "Will you marry me?"

For a moment, time seemed to stand still. Serenity's gaze was transfixed by the ring, its facets reflecting the dancing flames around them. Her doubts, her suspicions, her burning ambition for justice – all of it faded into the background, overwhelmed by the sheer romance of the gesture.

"It's beautiful," she whispered, her fingertips hovering just above the diamond.

Cartier's lips curved into a tender smile. "Not nearly as beautiful as you."

Serenity's heart raced, her mind a whirlwind of conflicting emotions. She took a deep breath, steadying herself against the onslaught of feelings threatening to overwhelm her.

"Yes," she breathed, her voice barely audible. "Yes, I'll marry you."

Cartier's face lit up with genuine joy as he slipped the delicate beauty onto her finger. He rose to his feet, pulling her into a passionate embrace. As Cartier's lips met hers, Serenity's thoughts once again drifted to Lila, her childhood best friend. Would she approve of this decision? Or would she be disappointed in Serenity's apparent weakness?

"I love you," Cartier murmured against her ear, his warm breath sending shivers down her spine.

Serenity forced a smile, burying her face in his chest to hide the conflict in her eyes. "I love you more," she replied, the words tasting bittersweet on her tongue.

She tried to focus on the future, on the possibilities this engagement might bring. Perhaps this was the key to unlocking the truth, to finally bringing justice for Lila and perhaps Cynthia too. With Cartier's ring on her finger, she would have unprecedented access to his world, his secrets. Serenity searched for excuses to justify her decision to accept his proposal.

"You've made me the happiest man in the world," Cartier said, pulling back as they shared an intense stare, forcing Serenity to maintain her composure.

"And you've made me the happiest woman," she lied smoothly, or was it a lie? The lines had become blurred. Her heart torn with the potential consequences of her deception but also the guilt of truly falling in love with a man who was a monster.

Cartier sprinkled kisses along Serenity's neck and shoulders. In the dim light of the bedroom, she could just make out the outline of his muscular body as he led her to the bed. She could see the lust and love in his eyes. He slipped out his silk pajama trousers and Serenity savored in the perfection of his form. His lips soft, full and inviting roamed her body. She could feel Cartier's strong arms around her, his hands exploring every curve with tender yet possessive caresses. Her skin tingled under his touch, every kiss and brush of his fingertips driving her closer to a state of pure bliss.

Taking in the alluring aroma of his cologne mixed with the faint scent of vanilla from the candles scattered around the room, adding a sense of warmth and sweetness to the atmosphere. They reached the crescendo of their lovemaking, their bodies entwine in a passionate embrace, becoming one and falling asleep in each other's arms.

Serenity woke up, still basking in the memories of the romantic night before. At first, she wondered if it was all a dream until she saw the glittering diamond ring on her finger. As she shifted in bed, reaching for Cartier to snuggle back up with him, she realized he was no longer there. A note on the pillow explained that he had a business meeting and would be back later. But his words, "Love you my beautiful fiancé," made her heart flutter with joy. She couldn't help but repeat the word, "fiancé," out loud to savor its newness and significance.

She was about to order room service when Serenity glanced at her phone and saw a new text. The message read: ***I need to talk to you about Cynthia's murder. Meet me at the diner in one hour.*** She immediately tried calling the number, but it went straight to a standard voicemail.

Serenity hesitated, wondering if this could be a trap. But whoever sent the message knew about their usual meeting spot, which made her believe it was legitimate and she needed to go.

Serenity quickly pushed aside the warm covers and got out of bed, her mind racing at the mention of Cynthia's murder. She felt a surge of adrenaline as she hurriedly dressed, the events of the night before now a distant memory.

After leaving the comfort of the hotel suite, she drove to the diner, her thoughts consumed by what awaited her there. She parked her car and made her way inside, scanning the faces around her for any sign of who might have sent the mysterious message. She couldn't spot anyone who seemed out of place. Just as she was about to give up and leave, a figure in a dark hooded jacket and sunglasses caught her eye. Their face obscured by shadows. Serenity cautiously approached the secluded booth in the back, a figure stood with their face down. The figure gestured for her to sit down; their identity still concealed.

A familiar voice Serenity thought she would never hear again spoke, low and raspy. She looked up, her heart pounding in her chest. "You're alive." The words barely escaped Serenity's lips as tears threatened to spill.

"Please, sit down," Lila said quietly, gesturing towards the booth they were standing next to. She didn't want to draw any attention.

For a few moments, Serenity was too stunned to move. Then, she slowly made her way to the booth and took a seat. "What is going on?" she asked, her voice shaking with emotion.

"I know this isn't what you expected, but I think it's time you knew the truth," Lila replied.

"The truth about what? That you faked your death and this whole thing has been some sick joke?" Serenity's voice rose in anger.

"Serenity, please keep your voice down," Lila pleaded, reaching out to touch her hand. But Serenity pulled away.

"Don't touch me. I want an explanation for all of this," she demanded.

"I promise, I can explain everything," Lila insisted.

"Then start explaining."

"Cartier and Callie were trying to kill me. I kept getting sick and had to go to the hospital multiple times. No one could figure out what was wrong with me until Cynthia, who was my nurse decided to run some more in-depth tests. We realized I was slowly being poisoned."

Serenity recalled the email exchanges she had read between Cartier and Callie, discussing their plan to murder Lila. Poison was mentioned as the method of choice.

"So how did you go from realizing you were being poisoned to faking your own death?"

"Because I couldn't find any proof that Cartier and Callie were involved. I believed the only way to gather evidence against them was to make them think their plot to kill me had succeeded."

Serenity tried to process this information. "That's quite an elaborate scheme."

"It was necessary, and I couldn't have done it without help from Cynthia, and ultimately Bradley."

"Why did you involve me?"

"Because we had an unbreakable bond growing up together in foster care. I knew you would fight to get the evidence necessary, so there was justice for my death," Lila explained.

"But you're not actually dead."

"True, but Cartier and Callie still believe I am, and that they caused my demise."

"Why didn't you just tell me the truth?"

"I needed you to truly believe I was dead in order for this plan to work," Lila admitted.

"It was you that called Cynthia's phone the night I found her dead at the warehouse?"

"Yes. I didn't know who answered her phone. It wasn't until the next day when I finally spoke to Bradley, he told me she was dead and it was probably you I spoke to," Lila said.

"Now what? The evidence that proved Cartier and Callie's illegal activities and plot to kill you is gone."

"You forgot to include Cynthia's murder," Lila added.

"We can't prove that Cartier was involved in that," Serenity pointed out.

"Who else stood to gain from her death?" Lila questioned.

"I don't know, but..." Serenity began before her voice trailed off.

"Do you truly not know, or do you simply not want to know?" Lila asked, resting her eyes on Serenity's engagement ring. Serenity quickly placed her hand in her lap, forgetting she was wearing it.

"Bradley told me that you and Cartier had gotten close. I didn't realize you were that close."

"It's not what you think. It's complicated," Serenity confessed.

"I understand. Cartier is charming and knows how to say all the right things. It's easy to fall in love with him, but we both know what he's capable of. Do you really want him to get away with attempting to kill me and actually murdering Cynthia?"

"Of course not. But without evidence, there's no way to prove that Cartier was involved in either incident," Serenity stated defensively.

"Whoever has that USB drive is responsible for Cynthia's death. But maybe you're right and Cartier had nothing to do with it, however he still tried to kill me," Lila reminded her.

"I understand that." Serenity stated, sounding torn. "I should get back to the hotel. But Lila, I am relieved that you're alive. You have to believe me."

"I do. And I apologize for putting you in this difficult position. But I was genuinely scared for my life, Serenity. I believed that the only way to keep myself safe was by making sure Cartier and Callie were taken off the streets. They are dangerous and will do whatever it takes to get what they want," Lila asserted.

"How will we stay in touch?" Serenity inquired.

"I'll reach out to you again. But please, don't tell anyone that I am alive—especially not Cartier. When the time is right, everyone will know the truth."

"I won't say a word. I promise," Serenity reassured her as she stood up.

"Thank you," Lila said with a smile, hugging Serenity tightly. "I've missed you so much."

"I've missed you too," Serenity admitted truthfully.

"I hope to hear from you soon," Serenity said, turning to leave.

"You will," Lila nodded with certainty.

Serenity replayed her conversation with Lila as she walked to her car. She couldn't shake off the sense of betrayal lurking beneath the surface of her newfound knowledge. The conflicting emotions raging inside her. The rush of joy at seeing Lila alive warred with the doubts gnawing at her about Cartier and his involvement in all this. Serenity was lost and didn't know who or what to believe anymore.

Chapter Thirteen

Final Act

Serenity spent the next week struggling to compartmentalize her complex emotions. Learning that Lila, who she believed was dead, was actually alive had sent her mind into a tailspin. It also completely changed the dynamic of her relationship with Cartier. Unbeknownst to him, he was still a married man and holding onto a dark secret.

"Baby, are you not coming into the office today?" Cartier's interruption broke Serenity's thoughts as she sat on the terrace, trying to make sense of everything.

"I think I'll stay home and relax, if you don't mind. I'm not feeling quite like myself," Serenity replied.

"Is there anything I can do for you?" Cartier asked, lovingly kissing her hand.

"You've already done so much. I'll be fine."

"When it comes to you, it's never too much," he replied, gently caressing her hand. "Just relax and let me know if you need anything. I love you," he said placing a kiss on Serenity's lips.

"I love you more, Cartier," she responded, releasing her fingers from his hold.

Once Cartier left and she was alone, Serenity gazed out at the sprawling cityscape below. The gentle breeze carried the weight of her thoughts as she watched the city come alive from her terrace, the sun casting a golden hue over the skyline as if trying to warm her troubled heart.

Serenity felt the need to come clean with Cartier, but she couldn't help wondering if he would reciprocate. The longer she grappled with her thoughts, the more anxious she became.

Wanting to ease her mind for a bit, Serenity retreated to Cartier's library to grab a book to read. It was something she did often, as reading helped calm her nerves. As she perused the bookshelf, she noticed a few new titles, their spines protruding out further than the rest. She reached to push them back in place, but they wouldn't budge; something was blocking their movement.

"Hmm, that's odd," she remarked, removing a couple of books to investigate. It was then that she noticed a small compartment hidden behind the books. Her heart sank and a sense of dread flooded her when she pried it open and found the missing USB drive inside.

Serenity's fingers tightened around the USB drive as she collapsed to the floor. She struggled with her inner turmoil, feeling a desperate need to eliminate any traces of the past that could threaten her relationship with Cartier.

Tears streamed down her face as she held the USB, no longer able to lie to herself. The evidence had resurfaced to haunt her once again. In a moment of desperation, Serenity made a decision, she had to destoy the USB drive, and she needed to do it now.

Cartier sat confidently at the head of the sleek mahogany table in the conference room, meticulously reviewing his notes for the monthly board meeting. As Bradley and Callie, along with other members of the board, filed in one by one, Cartier greeted each of them with a genuine smile and a friendly nod. Once everyone was present, Cartier began.

"I would like to personally commend each member of our team on their hard work and dedication that has led to exceeding our revenue targets for the third quarter. This is a tremendous achievement."

He then moved on to discussing new goals for the upcoming quarter, outlining his ambitious plans for expanding and diversifying their product line. Bradley and Callie eagerly contributed their own ideas and suggestions, creating a collaborative and dynamic atmosphere. Together, they crafted a solid plan that would continue to drive the company towards success.

As the meeting came to an end with a round of applause, suddenly the conference room doors burst open and armed police officers and federal agents stormed in. The sound of gasps filled the room as everyone was shocked by this unexpected turn of events.

"Cartier Richardson and Callie Morgan," announced one of the agents as he slapped handcuffs on them, "you are under arrest for attempted murder, first-degree murder, corporate espionage, and racketeering."

Lila stood at the entrance of the conference room, a triumphant smile playing on her lips as she watched the room descend into a frenzy of disbelief and chaos as the gravity of the situation sunk in. Cartier's facade of composure cracked his face contorting in disbelief as he struggled against the restraints of the handcuffs. Callie's expression remained stoic, a flicker of something unreadable passing through her dark eyes.

However, when Callie looked up and saw what she believed to be a ghost staring back at her, her stoic expression vanished.

"Lila, you're supposed to be dead," Callie whispered in shock.

Lila victoriously declared, "You may have thought that, but unfortunately for you, like many other things, you were wrong."

Cartier's gaze locked with Lila's as if searching for answers in her veiled expression as the officers escorted them out of the room. The incumbrance of his sins and secrets bore down on the thriving empire Cartier had built but in an instant was in danger of crumbling now that he was going to prison.

As Cartier was led out of the building in handcuffs, it was the sight of Serenity standing near the elevator that crushed him the most. Her eyes were filled with tears as she watched him being taken away by the federal agents. He would never want her to see him this way.

Before disappearing into the elevator, Cartier declared his love for Serenity, leaving her heartbroken.

Meanwhile, Lila kept a safe distance and watched the emotional scene unfold. Once it was over, she approached Serenity.

"I know that was difficult, but you made the right decision," Lila lovingly reassured her.

"Then why does it hurt so bad?" Serenity cried, collapsing into Lila's arms.

"Because you're in love with him, but you will get through this. He is a monster, Serenity. You deserve someone much better," Lila said while comforting her friend.

"I have to get out of here," Serenity stated decisively.

"I'll come with you," Lila offered. "I don't think it's good idea for you to be by yourself."

"That's exactly what I want."

"Then I'll call you later and we can go have dinner and talk. Even though Cartier is gone, you're not alone."

"Dinner sounds good. Thank you, Lila. Your friendship means everything to me right now."

"You were there for me, and I'll be here for you," Lila vowed. "Let me go talk to Bradley. You try to relax, and I'll call you a little later."

After Serenity and Lila hugged goodbye, Serenity's heart felt heavy walking towards the elevator. As she made her way to the parking garage, she considered calling Audra for comfort and support. Audra wasn't in the office to witness the drama that had unfolded, but maybe talking about it with her would help ease Serenity's pain. She appreciated Lila's efforts, but knowing how she felt about Cartier, made it difficult for Serenity to share her true feelings.

Serenity rummaged through her purse, searching for her phone so she could call Audra. "Where did I put it?" she muttered in frustration. After a few minutes of searching, she realized that she must have left it in her office. She let out an exasperated sigh and headed back upstairs to retrieve it.

Serenity spotted her phone on top of her desk and saw a missed call from Lila. She considered calling her back, but instead decided to go directly to Bradley's office to see what she wanted. The building had cleared out quickly after Cartier and Callie's arrest. It was probably for the best; the media would be all over this scandal and everyone needed time to figure out how to handle it.

As Serenity approached Bradley's office, she noticed that the door was slightly open. From her vantage point, she could see Lila straddling him, although they were both fully clothed. Serenity stood closer to the door to eavesdrop on their conversation.

"Do you feel vindicated now?" Bradley asked.

"Absolutely. I put up with Cartier's cheating and lies for years. And when he got involved with Callie, his behavior only got worse," Lila exhaled angrily.

"Now you don't have to worry about that anymore. With the charges against Cartier and Callie, they're looking at life in prison," Bradley stated.

"And they deserve it. Plus, since I'm still legally married to Cartier, I'll inherit his entire empire. Everything is mine," Lila boasted.

"Who would have thought that sweet Lila was actually such a devious mastermind?" Bradley chuckled. "I have to give you credit - you pulled this off seamlessly."

"Thank you. Although I do regret that Cynthia had to die," Lila admitted.

"Yeah, but we couldn't afford any loose ends. And framing Cartier for first degree murder is much better than attempted murder," Bradley pointed out.

"That's true, especially since he isn't even guilty of that," Lila laughed.

"Speaking of loose ends, have you figured out what we should do about Serenity?" Bradley asked.

"I think we should keep her around. She has proven herself to be quite valuable," Lila reasoned. "Serenity is the one who turned over the USB drive. Besides, I'm sure the prosecutor is going to need her to testify at trial. We don't want anything to happen to their star witness."

"Very true. I must admit, planting the evidence in Cartier's library was a risky move. How did you know Serenity wouldn't destroy it?" Bradley wondered.

"Despite her obvious love for Cartier, I knew her conscience would compel her to turn over the evidence to the authorities. Even in foster care, she always tried to do the right thing - as if those people gave a damn about us. That's why when I decided to run away, I left her behind," Lila smirked.

"I adore your naughty side," Bradley whispered while caressing Lila's body.

"I don't think this is an appropriate place for us to engage in sexual activities," Lila giggled. "Someone might walk in on us."

"Don't worry, the building has been cleared out by Cartier and Callie's arrest. We're all alone here," Bradley figured.

"Well, when you put it that way," Lila smiled as she leaned in to kiss Bradley passionately. Soon, they began making love right there in his office.

Meanwhile, Serenity had heard enough. The deceit cut deep, and listening to Lila revel in how her conniving plan unfolded, had Serenity ready to commit her own murder. Even with the shock and pain raging inside her, Serenity managed to compose herself and quietly slipped away from Bradley's office.

Learning Lila, her trusted friend was the mastermind behind all this chaos that had torn apart her life was the ultimate betrayal. Serenity's thoughts then turned to Cartier. The image of him being taken away in handcuffs haunted her. Despite her intense desire for revenge, Serenity chose to be patient and keep her composure. She made a solemn vow to herself that she would seek retribution against Lila in a way that she would never expect, as true revenge was best served without any warning.

Mastermind

Serenity's Revenge...

Coming Soon

A KING PRODUCTION
Stackin' PAPER VIII
No Way Out...
A Novel
JOY DEJA KING

A KING PRODUCTION
Bitch
The Story Of Precious Cummings
MOVIE EDITION
A Novel
JOY DEJA KING

Started From The Bottom

Coming from nothing and having nothing are two different things. Yeah, I came from nothing, but I was determined to have it all. And how couldn't I?

I exploded into this world when hood rich wasn't an afterthought, but the only thought. You turn on the television or go on social media and every nigga is iced out with an exotic whip, surrounded by a bitch in a G-string, bundles down to her ass, poppin' that booty. So, the chicks in videos were dropping it like it's hot for the rappers, singers and athletes, while the bitches around my way were dropping it for our own super-stars. Dealing with a street nigga on a legendary drug kingpin status was like being Beyonce herself on Jigga Man's arm. A bitch like me was thirsty for that. I'd been on some type of hustle since I was in pampers. I grew up in the grimiest Brooklyn projects. It was worse than being in prison because you knew there was something better out there; you just didn't know how to get it. You never saw green grass or flowers blooming. Instead of looking up to teachers, lawyers, or doctors, you worshipped the local drug dealers who hustled to survive and escape their existence. Even as a little girl, I knew I wanted more out of life. Somehow hustling was in my blood.

First, I hustled for my moms' attention because she was too busy turning tricks to pay me any mind. I never knew who my daddy was, so while my mom was fucking in her bedroom, I would wait outside the door with my legs crossed, holding my favorite teddy bear in one arm as I sucked my thumb. When the tricks would come out, I would look at them with puppy-dog eyes and ask, "Are you, my daddy?" The question would freak them out so badly they'd toss me a few dollars so I would shut the fuck up.

One day when I was five, my mother was looking for something in my drawers, she came across a bunch of fives and tens and some twenties. The total was five hundred and some change. Of course, she wanted to know where all the money came from. When I told her that the money came from her business clients (that's what my mom called them), she lit up. She tossed me up in the air and said, "Baby, you my good luck charm. I knew one day you'd make me some money."

On that rare occasion she showed me mad love.

As young as I was, I equated my mother's newfound interest in me with love. From that moment on, I learned how to hustle for my moms' attention, by providing her with money.

Somehow, my moms' customers never messed with or tried to fondle me. I think it's because even as a little girl I had this darkness in my eyes, that said, "Don't fuck wit' me."

By the time I was fifteen with all the tricks my mom's pulled, we were still dead ass broke, living in the projects. She couldn't save a dime because with hooking comes drugging and my mom's stayed high. I guess that's all you can do to escape the nightmare of having all types of nasty, greasy fat motherfuckers pounding your back out every damn day. The characters that I saw coming in and out of our apartment were enough to make me want to sew up my pussy so nobody could get between my legs, but my mother would soon change all that.

One day, I was sitting at home watching a weekly vlog on YouTube from one of my favorite social media influencers. She was doing beauty maintenance and self-care. I was completely caught up that I almost didn't hear my mother's bedroom door open. I heard the floor squeak and immediately turned off the television. Without a word, I started giving the living room a lick and a promise. I emptied several full ashtrays, picked up the dirty glasses scattered about the floor and wiped off the cocktail table.

Out of the corner of my eye, I watched my mother stare at me for a few minutes. She had the strangest look on her face. She was holding a bottle of whiskey in one hand and a cigarette in the other. My mother was only 33 but living a reckless life filled with drugs and heavy drinking had taken its toll. With unkept hair, poor hygiene, and a nasty disposition, most of the time I couldn't stand being around her. There was no trace of the once curvy beauty that every hood chick envied. Her once long, wavy hair was now thin and straggly. The one-time ghetto queen was just a bag of bones that you wouldn't even recognize unless you stared deeply into the green eyes she inherited from her father.

It was the middle of the afternoon, and she was just waking up, still wearing her dingy nightgown, blowing smoke in the air. She held on tightly to her cigarette, staring at me as if I was a reminder of what she used to be in her prime.

"Precious, you sure are growing up to be a pretty girl." I stayed silent and continued picking up clothes that were scattered on the floor and then started sweeping. "Didn't you hear what yo' mama said?"

"Yes, I heard you."

"Well, you betta say thank you."

"Thank you, ma."

"You welcome, baby."

My mother walked over to the couch and sat down with her legs spread open. She took one last long pull from her cigarette and put it out in the ashtray. She then took a swig from the whiskey bottle. The alcohol was spilling down her chin.

"Baby, you know that your mother is getting up there in age. I can't put it down like I used to. So baby, I was thinking maybe you need to start helping me out a little more."

Her comment made me pause and frown up my face. "Help you out more how? I basically give you my whole paycheck."

"Like I said, yo' mama can't put it down like I used to."

That bullshit made me stop sweeping the floor and I stared directly in my mother's eyes.

"What does any of that have to do wit' me? I barely go to school as it is because what was supposed to be a parttime job at the car detailing shop is more like fulltime. Damn near every cent I make, goes in your pocket to pay bills."

"Baby, that little job you got ain't bringing home no money. It's just enough to maintain. I'm talking about getting a real job."

I started sweeping the floor again wanting to ignore the foolishness coming out her mouth.

"Ma, I'm fifteen. It's only so many jobs I can get and so much money I can make. My boss not even supposed to give me all the hours she has me doing at the shop. That's why she pays me off the books."

"Precious, as pretty as you are you can be making thousands of dollars."

"Doing what? What job you know is going to pay a fifteen-year-old high school student thousands of dollars?"

"The oldest profession in the book...sex."

"You said that as if you asking me to do something as innocent as baking cookies for a living. You done lost yo' damn mind. What you tryna be now—my pimp!"

"You betta watch yo' mouth, little girl. I'm yo' mama. Don't forget that."

"Don't you forget it! You must have if you asking me to sell my ass so I can take care of you."

"Not me—us. Shit, I took care of yo' ass for the last fifteen years. Breaking my back and wearing out my pussy to provide us with a good life."

"This is what you call a good life?" I twirled the wooden handle of the broom around the living room as I looked at the cluttered two-bedroom apartment. The hardwood floors were heavily scratched with a few roaches crawling near the entrance to the kitchen. Visible holes in the walls and decaying window frames with cracks in the glass. My mother stood up real defiant like and pointed her finger at me.

"You listen here, a lot of these children around this way don't even have a place to stay. It might not be much to yo' ungrateful ass but it's mine."

"That's a lie. You don't even own this raggedy-ass apartment." We stared each other down for a few moments because I wasn't budging. "Sorry to disappoint you, but I'm not following in your footsteps by selling my pussy to some low-down niggas for money," I made clear then shrugged my shoulders brushing the bullshit off.

"Well then you betta start looking for someplace to live, 'cause I can't support both of us."

"You tryna tell me you would put me out on the streets!"

"You ain't leaving me a choice, Precious. If you can't bring home some extra money, then I'll have to rent out your bedroom to pay the bills."

"Who gon' pay for that piece of shit of a room?"

"Listen, I ain't 'bout to sit up here and argue wit' you. Either you start bringing home some money or find another place to live. It's up to you. But if you don't give me a thousand dollars by the first of the month, I need you out by the second."

"How the fuck am I supposed to come up wit' a thousand dollars by the first of the month?"

"I told you. You betta start using what's between your legs." My trifling mother then cut her eyes at my vagina before her skeletal body disappeared into her dungeon of a bedroom. She was practically sentencing me to the homeless shelter. There was no way I could give her a thousand dollars a month unless I dropped out of high school and worked fulltime at the detail shop. But what made this so fucked up was this had nothing to do with the monthly bills because she had subsidized housing and received plenty of other help from the government. My mother basically wanted me to pay for her out-of-control drug habit.

Because the street life had beaten my mother, she wanted to beat me over the head with bullshit. But I refused to let that happen. I would hustle up that money, but I would do it my way. I was going to pick and choose who was able to play between my legs. My job at the car detailing shop was the perfect place for me to start. Nothing but top-of-the-line hustlers parlayed through, and one of them would be mine.

P.O. Box 912
Collierville, TN 38027

www.joydejaking.com
www.twitter.com/joydejaking

ORDER FORM

Name:
Address:
City/State:
Zip:

QUANTITY	TITLES	PRICE	TOTAL
	Bitch	$17.99	
	Bitch Reloaded	$17.99	
	The Bitch Is Back	$17.99	
	Queen Bitch	$17.99	
	Last Bitch Standing	$17.99	
	Superstar	$17.99	
	Ride Wit' Me	$17.99	
	Ride Wit' Me Part 2	$17.99	
	Stackin' Paper	$17.99	
	Trife Life To Lavish	$17.99	
	Trife Life To Lavish II	$17.99	
	Stackin' Paper II	$17.99	
	Rich or Famous	$17.99	
	Rich or Famous Part 2	$17.99	
	Rich or Famous Part 3	$17.99	
	Bitch A New Beginning	$17.99	
	Mafia Princess Part 1	$17.99	
	Mafia Princess Part 2	$17.99	
	Mafia Princess Part 3	$17.99	
	Mafia Princess Part 4	$17.99	
	Mafia Princess Part 5	$17.99	
	Boss Bitch	$17.99	
	Baller Bitches Vol. 1	$17.99	
	Baller Bitches Vol. 2	$17.99	
	Baller Bitches Vol. 3	$17.99	
	Bad Bitch	$17.99	
	Still The Baddest Bitch	$17.99	
	Power	$17.99	
	Power Part 2	$17.99	
	Drake	$17.99	
	Drake Part 2	$17.99	
	Female Hustler	$17.99	
	Female Hustler Part 2	$17.99	

QUANTITY	TITLES	PRICE	TOTAL
	Female Hustler Part 3	$17.99	
	Female Hustler Part 4	$17.99	
	Female Hustler Part 5	$17.99	
	Female Hustler Part 6	$17.99	
	Princess Fever "Birthday Bash"	$6.00	
	Nico Carter The Men Of The Bitch Series	$17.99	
	Bitch The Beginning Of The End	$17.99	
	Supreme...Men Of The Bitch Series	$17.99	
	Bitch The Final Chapter	$17.99	
	Stackin' Paper III	$17.99	
	Men Of The Bitch Series And The Women Who Love Them	$17.99	
	Coke Like The 80s	$17.99	
	Baller Bitches The Reunion Vol. 4	$17.99	
	Stackin' Paper IV	$17.99	
	The Legacy	$17.99	
	Lovin' Thy Enemy	$17.99	
	Stackin' Paper V	$17.99	
	The Legacy Part 2	$17.99	
	Assassins - Episode 1	$12.99	
	Assassins - Episode 2	$12.99	
	Assassins - Episode 3	$12.99	
	Bitch Chronicles	$40.00	
	So Hood So Rich	$17.99	
	Stackin' Paper VI	$17.99	
	Female Hustler Part 7	$17.99	
	Toxic...	$12.99	
	Stackin' Paper VII	$17.99	
	Sugar Babies...	$12.99	
	Deadly Divorce...	$12.99	
	The Legacy Part 3	$17.99	
	BITCH The Story of Precious Cummings	$17.99	
	Mastermind	$12.99	

Shipping/Handling (Via Priority Mail) $9.85 1-3 Books, $18.40 4-10 Books. For 11 or more $24.75.
Total: $__________FORMS OF ACCEPTED PAYMENTS: Certified or government issued checks and money Orders, all mail in orders take 5-7 Business days to be delivered